# ASSASSIN

"One of the greatest difficulties is writing convincingly from both an adult's and child's point of view, but [Myers] carries off the project credibly."
—*Booklist*

"Through the device of a fictional young woman interacting with historical figures, Myers provides readers with a glimpse of the people, events, and surroundings of a dramatic time in history. . . . The novel offers a good opportunity for discussion." —*SLJ*

"Although most Americans know that John Wilkes Booth assassinated Abraham Lincoln, few know the details surrounding one of the most significant events in U.S. history. . . . Myers brings all of the characters to life, and readers will get a sense of the conflicting loyalties that many Americans experienced during the Civil War and its aftermath. This exciting historical novel will be popular." —*VOYA*

## Praise for *Tulsa Burning*

★ "In this emotional page-turner, Myers expertly captures an era of poisonous racism while conveying the strong, true voice of a courageous young man. . . . Compassion and hope prevail in a powerful novel."
—*Booklist*, starred review

## Praise for *Hoggee*

"Fine, simply told historical fiction." —*Kirkus Reviews*

## ALSO BY ANNA MYERS

*Red-Dirt Jessie*

*Rosie's Tiger*

*Graveyard Girl*

*Fire in the Hills*

*Spotting the Leopard*

*The Keeping Room*

*Ethan Between Us*

*Captain's Command*

*When the Bough Breaks*

*Stolen by the Sea*

*Tulsa Burning*

*Flying Blind*

*Hoggee*

*Confessions from the Principal's Chair*

*Wart*

# ASSASSIN

## ANNA MYERS

Walker & Company

New York

First published in the United States of America in 2005 by
Walker Publishing Company, Inc.
Paperback edition published in 2007
Distributed to the trade by Holtzbrinck Publishers

For information about permission to reproduce selections from
this book, write to Permissions, Walker & Company,
104 Fifth Avenue, New York, New York 10011

Library of Congress Cataloging-in-Publication Data available upon request
LCCN: 2005042275
ISBN-13: 978-0-8027-8989-1 • ISBN-10: 0-8027-8989-7 (hardcover)
ISBN-13: 978-0-8027-9643-1 • ISBN-10: 0-8027-9643-5 (paperback)

Visit Walker & Company's Web site at www.walkeryoungreaders.com

Book design by Ellen Cipriano
Book composition by Coghill Composition Company
Printed in the U.S.A. by Quebecor World Fairfield
2 4 6 8 10 9 7 5 3 1

All papers used by Walker & Company are natural, recyclable products
made from wood grown in well-managed forests. The manufacturing processes
conform to the environmental regulations of the country of origin.

## TO GRACE ANN MYERS

You were the most beautiful newborn I'd ever seen. Although your birth was a normal one, with the aid of instruments, you had none of the redness or misshapen features of most newborns. Your beautiful, sweet face reminded us of a rosebud, and your papa John accidentally called you "Rose" several times that first day. You are not the only Grace Myers in our family. Your aunt Grace, sister of your grandfather who is in heaven, came before you. I hope you will grow up with the same gentle spirit of Grace Myers Scrivener. I also hope you will have the graceful, poised style of your mother and your grandmother Nelda. There are many strong women in the histories of your family, and I am confident that you will grow to be one of them. Welcome to the world, little rosebud. I thank God for the joy of having a granddaughter. We all love you and thrill to your adorable smiles.

*—Nana*

## FOR MY DAUGHTER

You are small
So too is the breath that
wraps the strongest word.

Nine months you grew upside down
like a potted onion in the womb;
we waited for you like
the tune waits for the word.

Child, when the geese dote upon
some puddle of sky above the
chilling lake, look on them as words.

Your face to your mother's is as
the leaf to the tree,
her love to yours as
the thought to the word.

I was a beginning once as
you are a beginning now.
Every period leaves behind it
a space for the coming word.

—*Ben Myers*

# ASSASSIN

# Prologue

It is twilight in Richmond, Virginia. The year is 1859. A woman in a lovely green gown walks toward a theater. She holds the hand of her daughter who is eight years old. The little girl has thick black curls and a round sweet face.

A young actor comes from a different direction and reaches the theater door just as the mother and daughter do. He is in the play and should be already behind the curtain where his makeup will be applied. His impulse is to push in front of the woman and child, to open the door and hurry inside. He does not. He is, after all, a gentleman. The makeup can wait. He holds the door for the mother and daughter. His eyes meet the eyes of the girl. They smile at each other, and he thinks what a beautiful child she is.

The young actor is John Wilkes Booth. At twenty he is not really famous, but he will be. Before he is twenty-five, he will be called the most handsome man in America. He will be the first performer to have his clothing partially torn off by his female fans. Before he is twenty-seven, he will be dead, his name despised. The actor's brother, Edwin, who is also an actor, will never speak his name again, but Edwin will die with his brother's picture beside his bed.

The girl will remember seeing the young actor on the theater steps and in the play. He will not remember her, but she will tell him about their meeting when their paths cross again. He will bring her much pain. Here are their stories.

# 1

# BELLA

## HER STORY

———◆———

I am not evil. I tell this story so that you might understand and perhaps so that I might see more clearly. I was
christened Arabella Getchel, but I have always been
called Bella. He was the first to say I should be addressed
by my full given name. On the lips of John Wilkes Booth,
Arabella sounded like a name fit for an angel. I have used
his full name as the newspapers do, but I have not forgotten that he liked to leave off John, liked to be called
Wilkes. He is dead now, and people everywhere say he
was vile. Still, I cannot bring myself to go against his
wishes. History will use his full name, but in the rest of
my story and in my heart he will be, always, Wilkes.

When I was but little, my mother clothed me in frilly
dresses. "You're a beauty, Bella," she would say as she

brushed my thick, dark hair, then tied it with bright ribbons to match my dress. She began very early to tell me that I was made for the stage, and she would take me to the Richmond Theatre often. I did not always understand the play, but I did love the velvet chairs and the applause.

My mother had a small stage built into my schoolroom, and there I would recite nursery rhymes and sing little songs for my mother and my tutor. Sometimes my father would be part of my audience. On those occasions, I tried to stand taller and speak more clearly. "Princess Bella," my father would call as he clapped his hands. Then he would lift me high into the air, and my curls would bounce against my head.

When my mother lay dying from consumption, she called me to her bedside. "The theater, Bella," she whispered through fever-dried lips. "Don't forget the theater. I was never able to be on the stage, but you have the looks of a star." She stroked my hair until someone came and led me away.

My mother met my father in the theater. Mother was only a flower girl, selling her blossoms to gentlemen for their ladies. My father had brought a lady with him. I suppose he did give the rose to her, but when the play was over, he made some excuse to send her home alone in the hansom cab he hired for her. Then my father went back into the theater to find my mother.

Wilkes's father met his mother the same way. That theater was in London, though, and Wilkes's father was an actor, not the son of a cotton merchant, as was my own father.

Still, I found it extraordinary, when first I heard his story, to think that our parents met the same way. He told the story in the costume shop of Ford's Theatre, where I sat sewing a hem into a coat he would wear that evening. Others were present, the chief mistress of the costume shop, another actor, and the lovely lady who had come into the shop on Wilkes's arm. I did not remark at that time on the fact that my parents had met under exactly the same circumstances. My speaking at all would have been totally inappropriate, for I was only a poor girl who was allowed, occasionally, to sew in exchange for tickets.

My grandmother did not believe in the theater. She thought all actors were drunkards, and all actresses were loose women. Even though I, at fourteen, earned our living by helping the woman who was dressmaker for Mary Todd Lincoln, wife of the president, I was not allowed to spend a cent without my grandmother's permission.

Lest I be unfair to my grandmother, Cora Witherspoon, let me say that she fed and housed me from the time I was eight until I went to work at fourteen. I even owed my job to my grandmother, since she taught me the art of sewing and because she passed her White House position to me when her fingers became too stiff with rheumatism to work.

My father, Samuel Getchel, left me with my grandmother temporarily. Looking back on it now, I realize he began to forget about me even before my mother was buried. I stood beside him as the casket was lowered into the grave and squeezed his hand for reassurance. He did not squeeze back. He did not pull my body, shaking with sobs, to him. He only stood and stared.

As soon as my mother was in the ground, he loaded me, with only a small valise of my things, into our carriage and drove with me from Richmond to Washington City. "It isn't so far away," he said when I begged not to go. "Around a hundred miles, only a three days' drive."

No doubt we stopped at inns at night, but only after the hour had become very late. I had fallen asleep by then, and though I am sure my father woke me, my memory of that trip is only of the carriage. I did not mind so much by day and spent my time gazing out at the places we passed. But I do not remember what I saw. I remember only the night, the sound of carriage wheels on black road. Our coachman drove. Father sat beside me, but still I felt alone in the darkness.

It was late when we reached Washington City. My father, briefly aware of my presence, roused me from sleep when we crossed the great waters of the Potomac River. "Wake up, Bella," he said. "We are crossing the Potomac. It is an important river."

Eager to engage my father in conversation, I sat up, rubbed my eyes, and stared out at what I could see of the water. "Is this the biggest river in the world?" I asked.

"Oh, no," said my father, and he made a sort of bitter-sounding laugh. "It is a vital one, however." He leaned around me to peer out the window. "This is the Potomac. It forms the border between our own state of Virginia and Washington City, where men try to make laws that govern people, justly or unjustly."

I did not grasp the meaning of my father's words, but I was hungry for the sound of his voice. "Tell me about the laws, Papa." My eyes were heavy, but I did not close them.

My father sighed. "Not now," he said, "but I fear you will grow to understand them. I daresay even children will comprehend and tremble."

His tone was harsh, and I, unwilling to agitate him more, drew away from him to lean close to the window. I did not go back to sleep. Instead I stared out at the dark city, and soon the coach stopped in front of a small cottage. "Your grandmother lives here," said my father.

As Papa climbed down from the carriage, I thought I finally understood the reason for our journey. We had, I believed, come to visit my grandmother. I remembered then that my mother and I had made the journey maybe three years ago, when I was five. We had stayed in a fine inn, but we had come to visit my grandmother's small cottage. I remembered that she had made a beautiful dress for my favorite doll.

"Wait here for me, Bella," Papa said. In the moonlight, I could see him as he knocked upon the wooden door. I could not see my grandmother when she opened the door. But I heard her scream, and I knew my father must have told her of my mother's death. Very shortly, he came back to the carriage, took my valise, and helped me down.

Inside the one-room cottage, I looked around. In one corner was an iron stove for cooking. A cupboard stood against the wall near the stove, and a small wooden table with two chairs sat in front of it. There was a fireplace with a rocking chair pulled close, and against one wall I saw a small bed. Papa and I cannot sleep here, I thought.

Then Papa said, "Be a good girl, Bella," and I understood suddenly that he meant to leave me.

"I do not have all of my dolls, Papa," I sobbed when he moved toward the door. "I cannot stay here without all of my dolls."

My handsome father bent his dark head to kiss me on my cheek. "It is only for a brief time, Bella," he said. "I will be back to get you soon."

Again he turned toward the door. His gold ring shone in the lamplight, and I grabbed at his hand in an effort to keep him with me. "How long, Papa?" I asked. "How many days before you come back for me?"

"Soon, my pet," he said. He pulled himself loose from me and went out into the night. I rushed to open the door again, rushed to seize one last glimpse of him; but strangely, the moonlight was gone.

I stood in the doorway of my grandmother's house, straining for sight of him, and I listened to the familiar, lonely sound of the wheels of his carriage. Finally my grandmother came and shepherded me back into her dark little home. She hardly knew what to do with me. My arrival had been totally unexpected, and she had just been informed of her only child's death.

That first night my grandmother put me into her own narrow bed. I lay there and watched as she pulled her small rocker close to the fire. She rocked and rocked, her body bent slightly forward, her arms wrapped around herself. The rocker made a steady sound against the wooden floor, and that sound mixed with the soft sobs that came from my grandmother's thin body.

I do not remember when or how my grandmother acquired the cot that became my bed. I recall only the despair we both felt. Despite her pain, she provided for me as best she could. Each morning after our breakfast, she would prepare a simple snack for my noon meal. Then she would leave for her job at the White House.

Usually she would say, "I hate to leave you alone all day, child, but we do have to eat, now don't we? And of course I'm expected at the White House to clean and help the dressmaker who comes to make Miss Lane's dresses."

I was interested in pretty dresses. "Who is Miss Lane?" I asked.

"Why, she's President Buchanan's niece. She runs all the balls and such, him having no wife. You can see plain that I have to go, can't you, child?"

I would nod my head. In truth, it was no matter to me whether my grandmother went or stayed. I was just as lonely with her in the room as I was by myself. As soon as she was gone, I would open the door, settle myself on the threshold, and with my one doll in my arms, watch and wait for my papa's return.

It was early spring when first I came to Washington City, but I did not notice how the grass turned green or how the leaves came again to the trees. My grandmother warned me each day, "You must not leave the house, Bella. You could be lost and never find your way back home."

From my waiting spot I could see two cherry trees with white and pink blossoms, and I remembered the story my tutor had told me about George Washington chopping one down. I knew the big river my father had talked about the night he delivered me to this house could not be far away. I should have liked to see the river in the light of day, but I did not consider going out. It was not my grandmother's warning that kept me from straying. Rather it was the terrible fear that my papa might come while I was gone, find me absent, and leave, never to return.

The scene from my doorway changed. Cherries came to replace the blossoms. I watched as they were picked. I watched as leaves on the trees turned yellow, red, or brown. My father did not return.

Finally there came a letter from my aunt Ruth, Papa's sister. My grandmother settled herself at the small table, and I took the chair across from her. It was not a thick letter. I held my breath as my grandmother used a knife to slit the envelope, for it was addressed to her, not to me.

Her eyes moved quickly down the sheet. Then she looked up at me. "Your father will not be coming for you, Bella," she said flatly. "It seems he has taken to drink and card games. Your aunt says your grandfather's business is in ruin, that your father sleeps all day and will see no one."

Not a word came from my mouth. Nor did I cry. I swallowed back the tears that might have come, and I looked about me. So this was to be my life. I was to live here in this one room with this woman who showed me no warmth. It was as if my grandmother read my thoughts.

She pushed back her chair, moved around the table, and pulled me into her arms. "Don't fret, child," she said, and she swayed her body to rock me in her arms. "Granny will teach you to sew, and she will make you a new dress." She kissed the top of my head. "It's not so bad, little Bella. We have each other now, and I am glad that he won't be coming back to take you away from me."

Even my childish mind could understand the situation. Thinking my father would come back to claim me, my grandmother had been reluctant to love me and face another loss. After that day, my life changed.

# 2

# WILKES

HIS STORY

The girl remembered me, seeing me on the steps and on the stage. Ah, fair Arabella, I regret what happened to you. Truly I do, but I want the world to know that I could not have spared you. No, no, I couldn't. You were part of a plan, a plan much larger, much more important than a little girl, no matter how sweet.

Looking back, I think perhaps in some way the plan began there in 1859, the year Arabella saw me on the Richmond stage, the year of John Brown's uprising.

Yes, they said old Brown was crazy, and perhaps he was. Still, he was brave. I remember the day, November 24, 1859. The war had not yet begun on that sweet November morning, but there were movements in that direction. I came out the door of the theater. The bright light after the dimness stunned my eyes, but I saw that the street was full of soldiers. Two units of city militia were lined up, waiting to board trains to Charleston. They were going to join hundreds who would stand guard at the hanging of John Brown.

In October the old man had led eighteen men in an attempt to take over the state arsenal at Harper's Ferry . . . abolitionist fool. His plan was to steal guns, run for the mountains, and wait there to be joined by slaves. He believed they would come to him, come running, those darkies.

He killed some soldiers and took a few men prisoner. Some of Brown's men died too, and he was captured. Such men always are. I wonder if old Brown knew that, knew that he was bound to die. Many simpletons in the North thought he should have been forgiven because he was insane, and there was also talk that some sympathizers might try to save him.

Hence the street in front of my theater was filled with militia. Suddenly I was struck with an idea. Why not join them? Why not be part of the men who stood for what I, too, believed? Death to those who try to change things in the South! Death to those who hate slavery!

"Wait," I called to them, and a group of five or so men stopped to look at me. "I'd like to join you for a bit."

One of them was younger than the others, but he was the one who spoke first. He peered hard into my face. "Aren't you that actor fellow, Booth?"

I smiled at him. "I am that same fellow," I say, "but I've a notion to join your noble band for a time if you could get me a uniform."

"Who would do your part in the show?" He pointed with his gun toward the show card with my name posted outside the theater.

"I don't know." I laughed. "Nor do I care if I can but be one of you, and I would gladly pay for a uniform."

One of the older ones spoke more to his fellow soldier than to me. "We could get one off the sarge, I'd wager."

The young one nodded his head. "Yes," he said to me. "Will it be blue or gray for you?"

I did not hesitate. Had I not worn the gray uniform in school? "Gray," I said with a thrill. "It is always gray for me."

Strange how those words ring in my ears and rest now in my heart, Gray, gray for me. We traveled to Charleston, a fine city, ruined later because it became the capital of West Virginia, that traitorous state that broke away from the true Virginia when it nobly seceded from the union. How could the people there choose so? How could they desire to stay part of a country run by a man such as Lincoln?

But not knowing what lay ahead for the area, I found it pleasurable. We camped outside the city for eight nights. I lived there with the soldiers and was truly one of them. At night we gathered about the fire, comrades all. We sang "Old Dan Tucker," and other good old camp songs. Then a soldier with a beautiful tenor voice sang "Danny Boy," a song about a father whose son is leaving home. The haunting melody made me think of my own father.

"My beautiful boy," my father used to call me. He was a man who did not live by rules made by other people. He left his first wife and son in England, brought my mother to America, and had ten children with her. My parents were finally married on my thirteenth birthday, two years before my father's death. As I listened to the song, I thought that I, like my father, must make my own rules for life. "You are a Booth, boy," he often told me.

When the song was over, they began to call for me. "Booth, Booth," they chanted, and of course I did not disappoint them. I stood and did readings for them, playing Henry from *Henry III*, Brutus from *Julius Caesar*, and Lear from *King Lear*. Ah, how they applauded, the sweetest applause, perhaps of my career . . . and cheers too. They cheered me for wanting to be one of them.

A newspaperman recognized me and wrote about me, saying I was not a member of their group, but that when I heard their drum roll, I felt compelled to join. It is true! I did have the feeling that I must be one of them, must express my loyalty to the South.

On the morning of December 2, we lined up around the scaffold. It was a brisk day, but not over cold for the time of year. There must have been well over a thousand of us uniformed men there. No civilians were allowed to watch, for fear of trouble, and I felt fortunate to be an observer.

John Brown was escorted from the jail to the wagon by a man named Avis who had been his keeper for seven weeks. Avis, they say, had grown to like Brown, and the old man gave the jailer his silver watch in appreciation of the kind care he had received. He also gave him a note all about how it would take blood to wash away the crime of slavery. Poor old soul, he really believed slavery was wrong. Did he not see that the colored man was better off as a slave, that this country was made for the white man?

We could see him come riding up to the field outside of town where the gallows had been prepared. He sat on a long wooden box, his coffin, and jumped from the wagon with more ease than would be expected from one of almost sixty years.

From the gallows he must have had a pleasant view of broad fields with cornstalks and white farmhouses, seen through the leafless trees of winter. Suddenly I felt my eyes fill with tears. I was only a few feet away. How his heart must have broken when his tired old eyes saw that no one had come to rescue him.

They put a white linen hood over his head, and I felt sympathy for him rush through my blood. Not sympathy for his vile desire to free the slaves, not disregard for the five lives lost on his account, but compassionate regard for the old man himself. He was brave, brave indeed . . . knowing that what he did might result in his own death, but caring for nothing save the advancement of the cause he believed in, however terribly mistaken.

I could see him stiffen just before the fall, but he did not cry out. Then his body was hanging there in the Virginia breeze. A colonel shouted, "So perish all such enemies of Virginia! All such enemies of the Union! All such foes of the human race!"

Hearing his words, I wondered. Did he not know that enemies of Virginia and enemies of the Union could not be the same, not for long anyway? Did he not know that old Brown was right about the blood, but wrong in thinking it would be only the blood of Southerners? Did the colonel not realize we were on the edge of war?

When I was about to leave with the soldiers, an officer who had been a hostage of Brown's at the arsenal came to speak to me. Because he had been among my father's many fans and appreciated my desire to join the troops, he gave me the spear old Brown had carried. On the handle was written, "Major Lewis Washington to J. Wilkes Booth." It became one of my most treasured possessions.

I went back to Richmond with the soldiers, and they were with me when I learned that I had been dismissed by the theater manager for leaving without word. Several of my fellow soldiers prevailed upon the man to change his mind, and he did so.

Yes, I think that seeing old John Brown being brave enough to strike against that which he hated may well have been the beginning of my plan to strike against the tyrant called Abraham Lincoln.

# 3

# BELLA

————◆————

I would no longer spend my days alone. "We must get you to a school," my grandmother said after my aunt's letter arrived. Just two days later she came home with news of a school run by Mistress Newby, a kind Quaker lady who would let me attend in exchange for the sewing Grandmother would do for her family.

I was excited as we walked to the school. There had been little chance for me to see much of Washington City, and I enjoyed looking about. Compared to Richmond, where I had always lived, Washington City seemed to have an almost unfinished feel about it. One street, I learned later, had a paved surface, but mostly they were dusty or muddy, depending on the weather.

The street Grandmother and I walked down had a

board sidewalk for a time, but then the boards ended, and we had to walk in mud. "Hold up your skirts," my grandmother called.

Having been taught only at home, I had never been in a school. I imagined a large brick building with children playing games in the yard. My grandmother turned down an alley and stopped in front of a low building made of white clapboard. There was not even a sign.

"Is this the school?" I looked about for a larger building, but Grandmother knocked at the door.

The teacher came, and as she and my grandmother spoke, I leaned around her, trying to see if there were indeed other children inside. "I'll show thee to a desk," said Mistress Newby, and I followed her inside.

Boys sat on one side, girls on the other. On each side of the room, four pieces of lumber made narrow desktops, and students sat behind them. There was room for three students at each desk. One spot on the girl's side was empty, and I knew that I would sit there.

I walked beside the teacher to the desk she had chosen for me. It was before I took my place that I first saw Steven Browning. He sat, of course, on the boys' side. I looked up to see blue eyes staring at me from across the aisle. I do not recall anything about the girl I sat beside that first day, but were I to close my eyes now, I could picture Steven exactly as he was, hunched over his book, but gazing in my direction.

For a moment, I was aware only of those penetrating,

icy eyes. The ice melted, however, when he smiled. I was too shy to smile back at him. Instead I looked down and ran my hand over the wooden desk in front of me.

"You will be shown how to walk to the White House when your schooling is over, Bella," Grandmother had said just before she left me. I had been too interested in seeing the inside of the school to ask who would be my guide.

"Steven Browning's mother serves with your grandmother, and he will walk with thee, Bella Getchel."

Dear, gentle, Mistress Newby, with her gray hair, soft voice, and simple dress. She treated me with special tenderness, due, I believe, to my shyness and my being away from my home. There was always an extra pat for my shoulder, an extra smile when I recited. I cannot bear to imagine how great would be the distress to that teacher of my childhood were she ever to learn what path my feet would travel when I was ten and four.

But that day when I was but eight I knew nothing of the future as I walked beside Steven on the dirt road that led us to the north door of the White House. He was the perfect companion for a shy child. I had already observed on that first day in our small schoolroom that the boy loved to talk. Often Mistress Newby would stop a lesson, look at Steven, shake her head slightly, and lay her finger to her lips.

I always shot a quick glance at the boy across the aisle. Steven would look down, sorry for his actions, but shortly he would forget. Head up and full of enthusiasm, he would make some comment to one of the boys.

As soon as I learned Steven was to be my guide, I knew I would not need to speak much. "Just come with me," he announced when we were outside. "The real name is the Executive Mansion, but everyone calls it the White House. I live there, you know, with my ma up on the third floor where the live-in servants stay."

I did not know, and I stared at him, amazed. This boy lived in the very same house as the president my grandmother spoke of with such respect. We walked quickly for a few steps, but before we were out of the alley, he stopped. His hand was on his hip. "My ma says you come from Richmond," he said. "That so?"

I nodded. "Well," he said, "I'll not hold that against you." I suppose my face must have registered some surprise, because he went on to explain. "I mean, I reckon you are one of them Southerners. You have any slaves in your house?"

I nodded again.

"Well, I'd not be telling folks that," he said. "We don't see as how that is right."

I nodded, totally unaware as to why on earth anyone should object to the fact that George and Sally served my father's house.

Steven began to walk, and I stayed up with him. He bent to pick up a small stone from the road. He examined it closely, then slipped it into the pocket of his pants. "I collect things," he said. Then his eyes returned once more to me. "How old are you?" he asked.

"Eight."

"I'm nine," he said. We stood still for a moment, looking at each other, taking one another's measure. I stood considerably taller than Steven. "Ma says I'll grow. She says my brother Joseph was short like me too till he hit about twelve." We were at a corner, and he turned to lead me down the edge of a wide road with many carriages. There was no sidewalk, not even a board one. Steven stepped around me to be the one closer to the road. "My ma says a gentleman is supposed to walk nearest the street," he said, "on account of you might get splattered by mud or run over by a runaway horse."

I leaned around him, looking for runaway horses. I wondered if they were common sights in Washington City, but I said nothing.

Steven noticed. "You don't talk much, do you?"

He did not wait for an answer, just smiled and continued. "That's all right. Mistress Newby says I talk enough for six people." He paused for just a moment, then went on. "I like you. You're right pretty. You are the prettiest friend I got. But then it is not so awful hard to be prettier than Jeb Wilson." He laughed at his own joke.

I smiled at him. I liked being called pretty, and I especially liked being called friend. That's what we were from that day on, friends. I look back on many things with a sorrowful heart. Perhaps the most sorrowful of all is how I betrayed Steven.

He led me that day into the White House. It rose high amidst the buildings around it, and we walked across a large area of grass and trees to reach the door. The man outside the door smiled at us. "She's with me," Steven said, and the man opened the door.

"It's mighty big," he said, "but I know my way around. We could go to the servants' quarters, but I reckon it's all right for you to go to Mr. Buchanan's library with me. That's where I usually go after school. He allows me to read his books. You'll have to be quiet." He laughed. "Reckon that's no problem for you. Likely you won't believe it until we're in there, but I'm quiet in the president's library."

I had thought my Richmond home to be large, but I had never been in a place so big as this house where the mighty president lived. It matched how I had pictured the giant's palace when my mother used to tell me the story of Jack and the Beanstalk. I half expected to see a giant on the great stairs.

I wanted to move slowly, to look all about me at the bright glass chandeliers, the deep dark shine of the wooden furniture, the fresh flowers that rested on almost every table, but Steven was in a hurry, and I did not want to be left behind.

He started up the wide, red-carpeted stairs. "I like the

library most of all." He stopped for a moment about halfway up and looked me full in the face. "I hope you won't mind me telling you right out, but the truth is I'm exceptional smart."

I nodded, and he went on. "Mr. Buchanan said as much to my ma. He said something else that is a marvel. He said I'm to go to college, said he would pay for it every penny. All I have to do is mind my studies." He smiled broadly. "See, this is the way of it. My pa used to work for Mr. Buchanan when he lived back in Pennsylvania, before he got elected to run the country. We all came with him here to Washington City, but my pa died. Now Ma works helping to keep things clean. Ma likes things clean, and I like reading books, so it all falls out pretty well. Joseph, my tall brother, he went back to Pennsylvania on account of he is sweet on a girl there. Say, do you know the name of that street out in front?" He pointed. "The one that is paved is Pennsylvania Avenue. Isn't that grand? Of course, you being from Virginia might not think so."

"Oh, yes," I said quickly. "I like Pennsylvania." I had never before heard of Pennsylvania, but I could tell by Steven's face that he loved the place. I wondered if he missed his home there as sorely as I missed mine. I longed for the flowers that grew in our garden, for the smells of a lavish dinner spread on the table, for my mother's kiss. Steven's father was dead, as was my mother, but there was no time to think about that. Steven had started up the stairs again, and I hurried after him.

We were well down the hall when suddenly Steven put out his arm to move me back against the velvety wallpaper. "The president is coming," he whispered from his spot beside me. I looked up to see two men approaching.

"Which one?" I whispered, but Steven pressed his finger to his lips to show we should not talk.

"Yes, John," said the taller man, "I feel certain we must be unruffled. We do not want to anger the South more. Things will settle down if we remain calm."

"I hope so, Mr. President. I do hope so."

I stared into the face of the man who was the president. I hoped he would not object to my presence in his home. When they were near us, the taller man looked in our direction and nodded his head in greeting. "Hello, children," he said.

"Hello, sir," said Steven. The men walked on, but we did not move until they had disappeared down the stairs. "That was him." Steven's voice was soft. "He runs the total, entire country of the United States of America, but he stops to speak to the likes of you and me, who are the children of his servants. He is a true, great man."

I nodded. "Do you know what they were talking about?" he asked.

I did not, and I shook my head. "Don't you know that the folks in the South are down on the folks in the North on account of us not wanting them to have slaves?" I shook my head again. "They say they can have slaves if they want to, and they don't see it to be any business of the rest of us."

"Is it?" I asked.

Steven stared at me, his face shocked. "Let me tell you, Bella. It is almighty wrong for folks to own other folks, no matter their skin color. You just ask Mistress Newby in school. She will tell you how the cow ate the cabbage."

I did not see what cows and cabbage had to do with anything, but suddenly I did remember my father's words about the laws made in Washington. "I don't think my papa likes the laws that get made in this city," I said.

Steven made a small sound of disgust. "Your father is a Southerner," he said. "Southerners are pretty much all bad eggs."

He had gone too far now. Friend or not, I was offended. I folded my arms across my chest and stood absolutely still. "If my father is a Southerner, then I am too. I don't think it is very nice for you to say we are bad eggs."

A look of surprise crossed Steven's face. "I wasn't intending to be unkind," he said. "I just had a notion that I ought to tell the truth. Mistress Newby says being kind is just as needful as being honest." He frowned. " I reckon it's hard to be both. I'm real sorry."

In my full memory there is no other instance when I felt that Steven Browning was unkind to me. He was sometimes stubborn, sometimes prideful, but never unkind. For two years, we studied together in the small alleyway building that was Mistress Newby's school.

When Steven was eleven, our teacher told his mother there was nothing more she could teach him. President

Buchanan had left the White House by then, but an educational trust had been set up for the boy. My friend was sent to a boys' academy, where he learned Latin and studied the classics.

My schooling ended the same year Steven left. From Mistress Newby, I did, indeed, learn to hate the idea of slavery. "Thee has a good mind, Bella," she told me once when we were discussing the growing unrest over slavery. "I can tell thee what I believe to be the truth, but thee must decide what is the truth for thee and not be swayed by the opinions of others."

Oh, if only I had learned that lesson from my dear teacher. If only I had truly learned to stand against the influence of others.

True to his prediction, Steven did grow, but it happened before he was twelve. Sometime during that last year that we studied together I began to notice that he was taller than I as we walked side by side to the White House. I don't remember when exactly it was, but at some point I noticed too that his face had grown to match his eyes. They were still large eyes, but their size no longer seemed to dominate his entire being.

During those happy school days, I came to think less and less of Virginia. I began to feel Washington City to be my home. My father, it seems, was able to pull himself together and go back into business. He even remarried. He wrote to me occasionally, always with a promise to visit soon.

For a few days after each letter, I would miss my father, and I would try to believe he would truly come to see me. Believing, though, became harder and harder.

During that first year my grandmother began to teach me to sew. "You have a gift, Bella," she said. I sat beside her, and I remember how I grew warm with the pleasure of her praise. "I declare I've never seen another body learn as you are doing. Why, I believe you might become a great dressmaker, far surpass your old grandmother and be a mantua maker."

I bit at my lip and did not lift my eyes to my grandmother's face. I had no desire to learn to make the dresses called mantuas. The bodice of the dresses fit tightly with pleats in the back that ran all the way into the waist. They had great full skirts that draped over large hoops. A room could be filled quickly by fashionable ladies wearing mantuas. I had no desire to spend my life making dresses for rich women who would fuss constantly about the fit of their dresses and believe they should not be seen twice in the same garment.

I dreamed only of the theater, but I had learned early on that my grandmother would allow no discussion of such an ambition. "That's nonsense," she said. I had been with my grandmother several months before I confided my ambition to her as we ate our supper of cheese and bread. "It's a sinful place. I never encouraged your mother in such foolish thoughts, and I won't encourage you." She cut a slice of cheese and handed it to me. "Besides, you're shy, child. Do you imagine you would enjoy standing on a stage talking to a crowd of people?"

I shrugged my shoulders and put the food into my mouth. I did imagine that I would enjoy it. I would not be speaking as Bella Getchel, a timid, tongue-tied girl. I would speak as a queen or a princess. On the stage I would be able to step out of myself and lead many interesting lives.

Looking back, I find it ironic indeed that it was my grandmother's instruction in sewing that allowed me access to the theater. Can I be sorry that ever I set foot in Ford's Theatre? Perhaps I should, but alas I cannot.

# 4

# WILKES

HIS STORY

It is true! I cannot believe it, but Abraham Lincoln has been elected president of the United States! There is no recourse now for the South. We cannot stay in the Union, cannot be led by such a man.

What will be my part in helping to build the new nation that must be formed in the South? War will surely come now. I have promised my mother I will not fight in a war, and she worries about the war dividing the family.

I let people believe that I was in on the capture of John Brown, have described the events so well that at times I myself believe that I was there. Well, I was there in spirit. I was there when they hanged the man. What harm can come by adding to the story? My soul is too large to have limitation set upon it.

I want fame, but do I want to be known only as a famous actor? My father was famous, but he was also a great man, loved by many. He died when I was fifteen.

My father died during the winter, so we were at our Baltimore home instead of in the country when the news came. He died while touring, and my mother traveled to Cincinnati to claim his body. When she returned, she had the walls draped with white fabric to cover pictures and mirrors.

The only decoration in the room where my father's body rested was a bust of Shakespeare, which seemed to look down upon him. I am certain Shakespeare would look favorably on the man who brought so many of his characters to life on the stage.

Great numbers of people came to pay their respects. Some of them were rich and important. Some were not. "Your father had a good heart," one shabbily dressed man told me. He leaned against my father's casket. "You see how it is, me a deliveryman, your father a great stage star, but we was friends. He always had an apple for my horse, carried apples on him to give to horses on the street, and he always told us drivers to be kind to the horses." He wiped his eyes.

Are sons not supposed to move beyond what their fathers have achieved? I cannot stop feeling that I must be greater than my father.

After Father's death, we had little money. He had made no provision for us in case of his death. I suppose

Junius Brutus Booth thought he would live forever. I think perhaps I believed he would also. I remember the strangeness of looking down at his dead form, trying to believe he would never speak again.

My older brothers, June and Edwin, were in California when Father died, and my mother told them not to worry about coming home. My younger brother, Joseph, was allowed to stay in school. We rented out our Baltimore home. Mother, Rosalie, Asia, and I moved back to the farm, and for a few years I tried to farm.

In some ways those years on the farm were good. Rosalie always stayed inside with Mother, but Asia and I passed many happy hours in the fields and woods. I loved riding my pony Cola through the countryside. Always, though, I was restless, longing for something I could not name. I remember going to Asia one day as she lay reading on a blanket spread beneath a large oak tree.

I leaned down to take her book from her. "Let us be happy," I said. "Life is too short to be spent moping."

Asia sat up and crossed her arms. "John Wilkes Booth," she said to me. "I am happy. It is you who needs to heed his own advice. What is it that troubles you so?"

I thought then, when I was young and struggling to make a life as a farmer, that it was the stage for which I longed. I believed that I would find contentment in the applause of adoring fans. I have not done so.

In the fall of 1860, I was in Montgomery, Alabama, playing to fans who loved me. I remember the parties most. I was the guest of honor in many a fine home. We were at dinner during one of those parties when the hostess turned to me and said. "We have just bought a fine new racehorse, Mr. Booth, paid dearly for him, I can tell you."

She was a pretty woman dressed in a gown of black and white, her fair hair piled high on her head. Her blue eyes danced as she spoke. "You enjoy racing, I assume," I said.

"Oh my, yes, Forrest and I both do, but we shall enjoy it more with this wonderful horse."

Her husband, Forrest, at the other end of the table, entered the conversation. "Tell Mr. Booth what you want to name the horse, my dear."

The lady laughed. She bent her head in pretended embarrassment. Then glancing up at me, her gaze coquettish, she said, "I'd like to name him John Wilkes if you've no objection. He is a handsome animal and fine. I am sure the mares adore him."

I laughed. "I would be honored, my lady," I said, and I lifted my glass for a toast. "To John Wilkes, may he race always to the front."

After the meal, I walked about the plantation with my host and hostess. The late afternoon sun was still warm. We toured the barn to see the horses, and we walked along beside the fields that lay beyond the barn.

"What a lovely scene," I said, gesturing toward the fields where the slaves bent over cotton. They sang as they worked, and their voices carried to our ears. I remember thinking that it was a picture in danger of disappearing.

Only a few weeks after that party, Abraham Lincoln was elected president of the United States. In a four-way race, he won only 39 percent of the popular vote, but was elected by a wide electoral majority. I was backstage when a fellow actor showed me the *Montgomery Advertiser*. Staring down at the headlines that announced the election, I felt tears roll down my cheeks.

The newspaper recommended that Alabama secede, and all about me voices echoed the sentiment. When I left Alabama shortly after the election, I knew I would not again come to the dear state as part of the Union.

I went from Alabama to a theater in Philadelphia. Although I played to appreciative fans, I did not find the people there as warm as the people of the South. My sister Asia had married a man we had known from childhood, John Clarke Sleeper. He was beginning to do well on the stage as a sort of low comedy actor, and he reversed his middle and last names, thinking it would not be good to be known as a Sleeper.

Asia looked beautiful on her wedding day, and I tried to be glad for her, but I had never really cared for the groom. I did love Asia's babies. She had two by the time I visited her in her Philadelphia home. She sat on a love seat, smiling, as I rolled with the babies on the floor. How I loved those sweet boys, loved to kiss their soft sweet skin and feel their small hands clutching at my cheek. Asia was with child again, and I remember looking up at her and saying, "You might want to name the next child after your younger brother."

"You think I should name the next child Joseph, do you?" Asia laughed, but she knew that I meant myself. Even then, though, I doubted her husband would agree to have his son named for me.

John Clarke had a small mind. Therefore I should not have been surprised to learn that he was a Lincoln supporter. On that first visit to their home after the election, I simply avoided discussing politics with the man. A few weeks later the peace was impossible to keep.

I was at dinner with Asia and John when a neighbor came breathlessly into the dining room shouting, "South Carolina has seceded. The Union has been destroyed."

"It was bound to happen," said John. "Others will follow, and they won't go peacefully." He shook his thick head. "The fools will push us to war now."

Without even planning my actions, I sprang to my feet and put my hands around his neck, wanting with all my heart to squeeze.

"Wilkes," Asia yelled, and she jumped to push at my body.

I came to myself, dropped my hands, and muttered an apology. Asia glared at me, and I could not bear to have her angry with me. "I am truly sorry, old man," I said to the idiot Clarke. "I suffered a moment of near insanity, I suppose. . . ." I looked down at the plate full of food in front of me. "Ever since fighting to capture old John Brown, I've been a bit unstable on the subject of the South."

Asia smiled at me sweetly and put her hand across the table to pat mine. "You should never have gotten involved in a battle, Wilkes," she said. "Your spirit is too fine, too fragile, for such things." She turned then to look at her husband. "We won't let political arguments divide us from family, will we, John?"

Clarke made a halfhearted attempt to agree with her, but I knew that day that the lines were drawn. The man who had never really been my friend was now my enemy.

Shortly after South Carolina left the Union, Mississippi, Florida, Alabama, and Georgia followed. I waited almost with my breath held for Virginia to make her move. I believed that my home state of Maryland would do whatever Virginia did.

# 5

# BELLA

HER STORY

❧

November 6, 1860, was a sad day for Steven and me, and, I think I can say, for the employees at the White House. On that day Mr. Abraham Lincoln was elected president. Our beloved Mr. Buchanan had not even run for reelection, but still we felt somehow that Lincoln would be pushing our president out. Soon there would be strangers living on the second floor, not friendly Mr. Buchanan and his sweet niece Miss Lane.

Oh, we had heard a plenty about the new president and his family, heard that he was ugly, uneducated, inexperienced, and downright vulgar in manner. We had also heard that Mrs. Lincoln was a sour woman, given to bad tempers and fits of depression. Talk was that most Northerners only voted for him because he was an abolitionist and would do away with slavery. It was a known fact that because there was no Republican Party in the South, he did not get a single vote in eleven slave states.

"Imagine that," I said to Steven. "We are to have a president that not one person in eleven of these United States of America voted for."

It was a few days before the inauguration, and we were seated on a bench in the back garden of the White House. Steven broke a twig he had been holding in his hand and shrugged. "Oh, well," he said. "We aren't even united now, not with seven states seceded. More of those hotheads are bound to go."

I wished I had not brought it up. Generally, I agreed with Steven's ideas about politics. It was natural that I should. I spent my afternoons with him in the most polit-ical home in America, and Steven was always ready to explain his ideas to me. Still, I could not but feel a certain discomfort when people spoke disparagingly of the South. I had only lived in Washington City for two years. Was I not, I wondered, being disloyal to my father, and even to my mother's memory, to listen to the South being criticized?

Steven knew me well by this time, and so observant was he of my every expression that I could never hide a feeling from him. "Oh, don't be glum, Bella. I know you can't take all love for the South out of you." He laughed and pulled at one of my braids. "Likely, I wouldn't much want you for a friend if you could forget your home so easy."

Even though we knew we wouldn't like the Lincolns much, we were still excited when Inaugural Day, March 4, came. My grandmother and Steven's mother were busy in the White House that day, but he and I planned to take in the ceremony.

We stationed ourselves early along Pennsylvania Avenue to see the two presidents ride by. The crowd was already thick, but we found an empty spot and waited. The March air was sharp. I had dressed warmly in heavy stockings, a long wool skirt, and a thick shawl over my blouse.

A lady who stood beside us complained to her husband of being cold. "Why you want to see him is beyond me," she complained. "They say he is downright homely."

"I mean to see the man," said her husband, and he took off his coat and put it over his wife's shoulders. "We come all the way here to see him. He's got a terrible job ahead of him, and I want to see his face, homely or no."

There were armed soldiers all along the street, and even more uniformed men with rifles perched in the high windows of buildings. I felt uneasy seeing all the guns and said so.

"How do you suppose Lincoln feels?" Steven said. "There have been all kinds of threats to kill him, you know. There are seven states out of the union already."

Finally, not long before noon, we caught sight of them

coming, first soldiers on horseback and then the carriage, open so everyone could see. They sat side by side. We had always thought of Mr. Buchanan as tall, but Lincoln towered over him. Steven pulled a piece of paper and a pencil from his trouser pocket.

"What are you doing?" I asked.

"I want to write down things, some of what he says and all," he told me.

"Why?"

"So I can study on it tonight, of course." Steven was too kind to add, "Don't you ever want things to think about at night?" I knew, though, that my mind, so simple compared to his, must seem a mystery to him.

"How tall do you suppose he is?" Steven asked.

I shrugged. "Real tall."

Steven scribbled, "How tall?" on his paper and stuck it back in his pocket. "If we want to hear anything, we'd better hurry," he said then, and we began to move quickly down the street. After a few minutes Steven decided we should run. I knew my grandmother would say it was not ladylike to run on a public street, but run we did, along the edge of the street, through puddles, through crowds of people, and through groups of soldiers.

I almost collided with a pig being chased by a boy, and Steven did run right into a small man who sold hot cider from a pushcart. The man tottered backward, but Steven grabbed him. "Excuse me, sir," he said.

Nothing was broken or spilled, but the man shouted,

"Ruffian!" and I looked back to see him shake his fist in our direction.

We could see the Capitol a long way before we got there. It sat on a hill, a huge white building that seemed to rise almost up into the clouds. Workmen's scaffolds stood all about it because they were replacing the old dome with a much higher one made of cast iron. We caught sight of the rough seats that had been set up by placing lumber on barrels, but they were filled. Crowds of people stood behind the seating area.

We stopped at the back of the crowd, but Steven was not satisfied. "We won't hear a thing from back here," he said. "We are going to have to work at getting up front." He took my hand and pulled me after him. More than once, I saw him use his shoulder to force people to move far enough apart for us to slide between them. One man removed his tall hat and swatted at us with it, but we pushed on, reaching the front just before the new president was sworn into office from his place on top of the Capitol steps. We stood at the end of the third row of seats.

"The other fellow is Chief Justice Taney," Steven whispered.

"Who is he?" I asked.

Steven frowned. "You know, from the Supreme Court." He had his paper and pencil ready.

I did not know what the Supreme Court was, but I could tell from the frown that Steven did not want any more questions. Mr. Taney gave the oath to the new president. Both men held up their right hands. "I do solemnly swear that I will faithfully execute the office of President of the United States, and will to the best of my ability, preserve, protect, and defend the Constitution of the United States, " Mr. Lincoln repeated. We were close, near enough to see the deep lines in his face. His bones were big and seemed to stick out almost through his skin. His eyes were sad, very sad, and kind. He was not ugly, not really, I decided.

He talked about how he did not intend to interfere with the institution of slavery in the states where it already existed. That, it seemed to me, was friendly toward the South. I thought those words should make the people in the South feel better, but he went on to say that the Constitution did not give states the right to secede from the Union, and that he would protect property and places belonging to the federal government.

I knew there had been trouble in some of the states that had seceded over who the forts and arsenals belonged to, the state or the Union. Toward the end he said there would be no conflict unless the seceded states started it.

When it was over, Steven wrote, "I like Mr. Lincoln," on his paper. He showed me the sentence, and I nodded my agreement.

We took our time walking back down Pennsylvania Avenue to the spot where we would take different directions. Grandmother had told me to stay away from the White House for a few days at least. Steven was to stay out of sight in the quarters he shared with his mother. "We'll have to see how things turn out around here," Steven's mother had warned. "You younguns are good to stay out of the way and all, but still, we'd better wait and see."

School was not in session for the first few days after the inauguration. I waited at home each evening for the bits of White House news my grandmother brought home. The Lincolns were a change for the household staff, a busy, loud family in contrast to the quiet Buchanans. "Those boys!" My grandmother shook her head after the second day. "I doubt they've ever been told to be quiet."

I looked up from the stitches on my sampler. I was very interested in Lincoln's sons. Robert, seventeen, was away at school. Willie, ten years old, was just my age. The younger one, Tad, was eight. "Have you seen them?" I asked.

"Seen them? They're everywhere, sliding down the banister on the front stairs, sitting on the floor, and leaning against their father's knee while he talks to government men."

I went back to my sampler. As I worked on the embroidery stitches, Arabella Getchel, age ten years, 1861, I thought about Mr. Lincoln, a man who liked having his children with him even when he was busy trying to run a whole country. I wondered if I would ever see my own father again.

The next day my grandmother came home with big news to share. I had peeled potatoes for supper, and she began to slice them into a pan on the stove for cooking.

"Mrs. Lincoln has hired a Negro woman as her chief dressmaker. Isn't that something? Folks whisper that Mrs. Lincoln feels so comfortable with slaves because she had them when she was growing up in Kentucky."

I stopped laying the table with plates and forks. "But this woman can't be a slave, can she?"

"Oh, mercy no, not in the White House. She'll be paid all right, a pretty penny, I would imagine. Elizabeth Keckley is her name, and they say she can make mantuas that can't be matched by anyone else in this city." Grandmother reached for a lid to put on her pot of potatoes. "I have a hope to learn from her, so as to teach you."

I never wanted to discuss my grandmother's plans to train me to become a mantua maker. "Are you angry, Grandmother?" I asked. "I mean, about being a helper to a colored woman?"

My grandmother did not pause in her work. "And why should I be angry? Me with so much to learn from the woman."

After a couple of weeks, my grandmother said it would be all right for me to come to the White House after school. Steven and I spent most of our time in the back garden or the kitchen, ready to help with some slight chore. We were there on April 12, the day war began.

We had heard at school about how the fort off the coast of South Carolina had been attacked by Southern troops. A man had come into our little building. He held his felt hat in his hand. Looking up, Mistress Newby had said, "It's my husband. Will thee please sit quietly, children?"

She moved quickly to the back of the room. We children stole furtive glances at the two as they stood with heads bent close. Our teacher's husband had not come to school before, and we knew something important must be the subject of their whispers. When the conversation was over, Mr. Newby stayed at the back, but our teacher, white-faced, made her way to the front of the room.

"A battle has begun, dear students," she said, and holding to the edge of her desk for support, she explained about Fort Sumter. "I fear we shall soon be at war. Go home." She closed her eyes for a moment. "Thee should go home and pray. Pray that this terrible conflict might somehow yet be averted." We made no movement. "Go," she said. "Go now."

Steven and I looked at each other. As we filed toward the door, even the very small children were quiet. I looked back just before going out. Mr. Newby had joined his wife, and both were on their knees beside the big desk.

"It was bound to happen," Steven said when we were outside.

I made no answer. Steven understood so much more about things than I did. We knew that he was about to finish with Mistress Newby's school. It had already been arranged that he would leave Washington City in the fall and travel alone by train back to Pennsylvania, where he would go to a boy's preparatory academy. I felt lonely just thinking of his coming absence, and now there was this war thing. I remember that we spoke but little on our journey to the White House that day.

Willie and Tad Lincoln were in the garden, Tad on the ground with marbles and Willie on a bench. We had encountered the boys a few times before and had spent one afternoon playing a game of stickball with them. The boys looked alike, both with round faces that I studied, looking for some resemblance to their father. I saw none, and decided it would be impossible to see anything of that worn face in the features of a boy.

I did notice that each of them was marked with one likeness to their famous father. Their unruly hair stuck up in all the wrong places. They both stood up as we approached.

"We can't go inside," Tad told us. "Even Papa said we had to go to our rooms if we want to play inside." He dropped back to the marbles he had abandoned upon our arrival.

Willie did not sit back down. He looked at us carefully. "Did you hear? I mean, about the battle and all?"

"Yes," said Steven, and I nodded. The three of us had just settled ourselves on the bench when the president appeared. Both of his sons ran to him, and he hugged them. "I needed a breath of air," he said.

Mr. Lincoln amazed me when he remembered Steven's

name from the introduction he had been given to the staff and their families. Steven smiled widely, and introduced me to the president. "Bella's grandmother works here too," he said. "Mostly helping with the sewing."

"How do you do, Miss Bella," he said.

My heart beat wildly, but I managed a little curtsy and said, "Very well, thank you, sir."

"I am glad you've come to play with my boys," Mr. Lincoln said.

"Papa," said little Tad, "will you have to go and carry a gun now?"

The big man mussed his hair. "No, son, I'll not go to war, but I'll have to send other men, young men."

"As young as Willie and me?"

"No," said his father, "blessedly I won't be sending boys as young as you two, but there will be some who are only as old as your brother Robert."

My grandmother had told me that Robert Lincoln was away studying at a college called Harvard. "That's pretty young," said Tad. "Robert's age is pretty young."

"Yes," said his father. "Pretty young." I looked at his face and noticed tears misted in his eyes.

"Papa didn't want war," Willie said when his father had walked away. "It troubles him awful bad." There were tears in Willie's eyes too.

During those early days, everyone said it would be a quick war. Mr. Lincoln made a call for soldiers to serve three months. On May 21, word came that Richmond had been selected as the capital for the Confederacy. I heard the news at the White House. I had come to the back garden to wait for Steven to come out before we went in to see Willie and Tad.

Steven called the news to me as soon as he saw me. "Well," I said, "I'm sure now that my father will be involved in the war. Nothing could touch Richmond so closely without touching him." I bent from my bench to study a small group of ants that moved near my feet.

Steven dropped to sit beside me. "Wish I was just a little older. I'd be in the army." He pressed his lips together hard and, forming a fist with one hand, struck at his other hand.

The thought horrified me. "That's silly," I said emphatically. "You're way too young to be a soldier."

"I'm almost twelve," he said. "The boys who strike the drums are not much older."

"But you aren't older," I said, "and you aren't going to be a soldier. You're going to be a student at a military school, that's all."

We sat for a minute without talking before he suggested we go inside. I told him I had developed a stomachache and had decided to go back home. After he left, I stayed for a time on the bench, thinking. I dreaded the day later in the summer when Steven would leave me to go to Pennsylvania to school. Now I wondered how I would feel if he were going away to be a soldier.

Then I thought of my father. I closed my eyes to

remember him, but I did not see him as he was when I was eight. Rather I saw him in a gray uniform. He would, I was certain, be a soldier. I walked home, hating the war that tore our country apart.

When our school term ended, Steven and I spent more time at the White House, often going up with Willie and Tad to the private rooms on the second floor or to play on the flat roof. We tried hard to avoid contact with Mrs. Lincoln. She was not a small lady, and the wide skirts she wore over big hoops made her seem larger. Sometimes she was pleasant, smiling and saying, "Hello, children. Willie and Tad certainly enjoy your company." The next day she might snap at us.

Someone gave the boys a small goat, and we spent many hours playing with her. She loved us all and would follow us anywhere. Once when we had failed to secure the latch on her pen correctly, Nanko followed us to the backdoor of the White House and pushed her way in behind the laughing Tad.

Mrs. Lincoln happened to be nearby and, hearing the commotion, came to see what caused it. She began shouting, at once blaming Steven and me. "Get that goat out," she ordered, "and you two urchins go with it." She grabbed an umbrella from a stand, and started to wave it at us. I ran, but Steven stayed, helping Willie pull the reluctant Nanko out the door.

Outside, we put the goat back into her pen. Willie reached through the fence to stroke Nanko's black-and-white head. "Don't worry about Mama," he told us. "She doesn't mean to hurt people's feelings, but sometimes her troubles make her cranky."

I wondered what her troubles were, but I didn't want to ask. Steven never held back a question. He put out his hand to pet the goat too. "What troubles your ma?" he asked.

Willie spoke softly, and I had to lean close to hear. "She worries about Papa, you know, people wanting to hurt him. She frets about what people think of her too. Folks never take to her like they do Papa."

I wanted to say that people would like her better if she didn't try to hit them with umbrellas, but I didn't. Willie went on. "There's talk that she favors the South because she grew up in Kentucky."

I understood what he meant. Kentucky, like Maryland, Missouri, and Delaware, had some people who owned slaves, but those four border states had stayed in the Union even though many residents were unhappy about not pulling out. I didn't think, though, that anything Willie said really justified Mrs. Lincoln's moods.

Steven said aloud what I was thinking. He pulled back his hand and stood up. "Your mother doesn't seem to try too hard to get people to like her."

Willie stood too. "Mama's good, she really is." He pressed his lips together before going on. "She is just not happy, not most of the time, even back in Springfield. It's a burden for Papa, but he is always kind to her."

That summer of 1861 gave Steven and me our last easy days together. The Lincoln boys were kept close to home, but the two of us roamed the streets of Washington City that summer.

The city changed in July. Evidence of war had been plentiful before, soldiers everywhere, but on July 21, a battle took place not far away near a town called Manassas that was on a creek called Bull Run.

Steven had been excited about it the day before. "Lots of folks are going over there in carriages to watch," he told me. "I wish I could go."

His mood was different when he showed up at our house the next day early, even before Grandmother left for work. It was raining, and when I opened the door, he stood on our stoop with no cap to keep his head dry, the water running down his face. "Did you hear them last night?" he asked

"Who?" I asked, and I stepped aside so that he could come in.

"The soldiers. I heard them, all coming back into Washington City. I looked out our window, and there they were in the rain, just filling up the streets, not in any order at all, just men from all different regiments. Our boys got licked, bad, and they had to run back here for protection."

My grandmother had been at the stove preparing our breakfast, but she moved to the table and sank onto a chair. "This war won't be over in any three months like they said." She leaned her face against her hands. "You children mark my words. We're in for a terrible long time."

Later, walking the streets of Washington City, Steven and I saw for the first time what war was really all about. There were wounded soldiers everywhere, bleeding around their makeshift bandages, limping and leaning on one another. They were blackened with smoke and powder, and they seemed so terribly tired, about to fall. Lots of schools and churches were turned into hospitals.

"It's like the whole city is wounded," Steven said as we wandered about, our eyes taking in the misery.

In a few days, though, we began to notice that the soldiers who were not bleeding were trying to forget their troubles when they had a bit of free time. We saw card games played under almost every shade tree. Signs on all the drinking establishments said, "No Spirits Sold to Soldiers," because that was the law, but the military men certainly got alcohol from somewhere. We saw them, even in the daytime, stumbling out of doorways, their arms around women in dresses my grandmother would have called shocking.

In fact, I did not mention to my grandmother how much time Steven and I spent on the streets of Washington City. "It's a wicked place I am bringing you up in, Bella," she would say to me from time to time. "An awful place for a child."

I did not think of the city as awful. I was fascinated by

the hurry and the crowds, and I felt great sympathy for the soldiers who might soon face death.

I discovered that Mr. Lincoln shared my attitude toward the city. Once when we were near the president's office, he came out just as a man was seeking to see him. "I am Reverend Harvey," the man said to the president. "I want to talk to you about the sin that goes on in our city." Reverend Harvey was a pinch-faced man who looked as if he had an unpleasant odor in his nose. "I shudder to think," he said stiffly, "what should happen in case of our Lord's second coming."

Mr. Lincoln laughed and clapped Reverend Harvey on the shoulder. "I wouldn't worry, sir," he said. "If the Lord has ever been to Washington before, I doubt he would choose to come again."

Steven and I liked Mr. Lincoln more and more. We also liked Mrs. Lincoln's tall, light-skinned Negro dressmaker, and it was plain Lizzie Keckley did more than just make dresses. When Willie and Tad had the measles, it was Mrs. Keckley who helped their mother care for them. "She calms Mama down," Willie told us. "Papa is mighty glad to have her around."

My grandmother liked Mrs. Keckley too and enjoyed assisting her. "You look at those eyes, Bella," she told me once as we walked home together from the White House. "You look at her eyes, and you know she's seen some things. She was a slave for thirty-seven years, hired out by her owner to make dresses for other women. That's how she got her freedom. The women she worked for helped her raise the money so she and her boy could be free." My grandmother shook her head. "Why, she told me"—she lowered her voice, even though we were alone on the street—"Don't you go repeating this, but she told me she was so light skinned because the master had his way with her mother. After she was sold away, the same thing happened to her, forced to lie with the white man who owned her." She shook her head again. "That's why her son is so light he could join the army."

"You mean they won't let Negroes in the army?" I asked.

"No, the president's afraid the border states would join the Confederacy if we let Negroes fight."

"My mother and father had slaves," I said, although I knew my grandmother had that knowledge.

"Your mother was a good person, Bella, and I loved her. Still, that doesn't make slavery right. Just think of a woman as fine and smart as Elizabeth Keckley treated like that."

# 6

# WILKES

❦

So the war has begun. There was no other way. I think often of old John Brown's words about blood. There will be blood aplenty! Some of the blood has been my own. A knot grew on the side of my neck, a tumor they said it was. I went to a doctor to have it removed, and his knife cut deep into my neck. The wound healed badly, leaving a mean scar.

I do not remember exactly how it came about, the story that I had served for a time on the field of battle and been wounded there. Ah, yes, it comes back to me. I was at dinner in a hotel dining room with a woman whom I had just met. She reached across the table and touched my neck gently with her fingertips. "Were you injured in battle, sir?"

What could I say? Maryland had surprisingly not seceded as Virginia did, but many a lad from Maryland crossed her borders to serve with the Confederacy. "I could not but serve where my heart lies, with the boys in gray," I said. It was a small misspeaking of the truth. Certainly, my spirit was on the battlefield daily!

"Oh," said the lady softly, "I do not agree with the Southern cause, but I can feel nothing but admiration for a man who fights for what he believes in."

Of course, there were many who would hear the story and declare it to be untrue. To them I would merely say, "You know how stories circulate about those of us in the public eye, and it does look for all the world like a bullet wound." I would laugh off the subject. What harm could there be in such a story?

I found it to be something of a challenge to win the hearts of the women of the North even while telling them I had fought for the South. Ah, yes, their lips spoke of their love for the Union, but their hearts could be won easily by Wilkes Booth, who made no secret of his love for the Confederacy. Such a woman was Lucy Hale.

I saw her first in a dining room in Washington City where she dined with a young man I thought I recognized.

"Is that young Lincoln at the next table there?" I asked my companion, a man who knew many people connected with the government.

"It is," said he. "That's Robert, the president's oldest son."

"Umph!" I made a disgusted sound, and my friend, who knew how I felt about Lincoln, smiled.

Through the first few courses of our meal, I watched the couple. Young Lincoln leaned eagerly toward the lady when she talked, and his face spoke clearly of his admiration for her. She was not a beauty, her features leaning toward thickness. Still, by the time they took their leave, I could see that there was a charm about her.

"Pray tell, who is the lady?" I asked as we watched them walk away.

My friend laughed. "Little difference her name makes to you, Wilkes," he said. "She would never look your way, not with your known allegiances. That is Lucy Hale. Her father is Robert Hale, a senator from New Hampshire. The man is a total abolitionist and a favorite of Lincoln's. They say Hale will be appointed as an ambassador when his term is up."

"Abolitionist, aye?" I raised my eyebrows in question. "And you think the lady would not find me interesting, do you?"

"Forget her, Wilkes," he said. "She has no need of a complication such as you, I am sure."

I did not forget Lucy Hale. Rather I made it my business to learn about her, and by asking about, I discovered that she lived with her parents in the National Hotel. Immediately, I changed my own place of residence to that same hotel. On the first day, I sat for a time in the lobby, as if waiting for a visitor.

It was not long before Miss Hale appeared. She was expecting a friend to come by, I heard her tell a clerk. She took a chair across from me. I pretended to read a newspaper that I had with me, but I watched her. Then I put the newspaper down on the chair beside me and looked directly at her. She smiled.

"Excuse me, dear lady, but I believe you and I have met. Are you not Elizabeth Jenkins of New York?" I said.

"I am not." She spoke somewhat shortly, but something on her face made me certain she was interested in pursuing the conversation.

"I beg your pardon," I said humbly. I dropped my eyes and held my tongue. It was not a long wait.

"I know who you are," she spoke rather peevishly, but I was certain it was a pretense. "I've seen you on the stage, and I saw you recently when I dined with a gentleman friend."

I stood and bowed slightly. "I am J. Wilkes Booth, a fact you seem to know. Won't you give me the honor of knowing your name?"

"A lady never engages herself in conversation with a gentleman unless they have been properly introduced," she said, but a smile had crept onto her lips.

"I am sorry, dearly sorry, to hear that." I looked around me wildly. "Surely there is someone about who can perform such an introduction?" I clapped my hands. "Ah, yes, there is Herbert, the desk clerk. Shall I bid him come to my aid?"

"No," she said. "I've never considered myself to be a lady." She laughed and held her hand out to me. "My name is Lucy Hale, Mr. Booth."

And so began an acquaintance, one that quickly grew into a true friendship. I found Lucy to be fascinating, far more interesting than any other woman who had held my attention in the past.

She did not adore me blindly as so many others had. Rather, she knew me with all my faults, but liked me anyway. I found myself more and more drawn to her. I remember one day as we picnicked in a park. We sat eating and watching some children, a boy of about three and his sister, who was only a toddler. Their mother and father sat on a nearby bench, and the children played about them, often coming close to our blanket.

"Would you like a strawberry?" Lucy asked. The little boy shook his head no, but his sister held out her chubby hand. Lucy gave the child the berry, and we watched the surprised look that came over her face as she tasted the somewhat tart fruit. "Children are a delight," said Lucy.

I told her about Asia's boys and the joy I found in them. She looked at me, her brows raised. "So," she said, "do you plan to be a father yourself one day, Wilkes?"

Suddenly, my heart seemed to stop. I reached for her hand. "It would be a joy," I said, "if my babies could have a mother like you."

She studied my face for a second, then shook her

head. "Oh, no, Wilkes, not I. It would never work. I could not turn my head while you played with other women."

"Why would I want other women if I had you?" I asked.

She shrugged her shoulders. "Why indeed, Wilkes, but you would, that I know. I know too that I would not put up with your roving eye. Besides, my father would hate my being married to an actor, especially an actor with Southern sympathies. We could never be married."

"Don't speak so," I pleaded.

"For all sad words of tongue or pen, The saddest are these: It might have been," Lucy quoted "Maud Muller," a poem by John Greenleaf Whittier.

"Save your sad poems, Lucy," I declared. "I will not accept a sad ending to our love."

Lucy was a bright spot during those first years of Lincoln's presidency, but still I counted the days until another election. For a time it seemed very likely that he would not be reelected. Many people, even in the North, called Grant the cigar-smoking butcher and condemned Lincoln for supporting the general. Besides, Grant had difficulty winning, and thousands of men were killed or wounded.

All that summer of 1864 there was a spring in my step. When I was in Washington City, Lucy and I spent time together, keeping our meetings secret from her father. I fell more and more in love with the only woman I had ever known who did not beg me to marry her.

Then in August word came of a Union victory at the

Battle of Mobile Bay, cutting the city of Mobile off from supplies. On September 2, Sherman's hard-marching troops took Atlanta. I hated the Northern victories, but felt even more miserable because those victories seemed to make Lincoln more popular.

The Democrats had nominated General George B. McClellan, and at first I had hopes that he might win. My hatred for the man Lincoln had grown as big as my love for the South, bigger perhaps. Lincoln won reelection by an electoral vote of 212 to 21, and a popular majority of more than 400,000 votes.

The North was filled with fools! I drank for two days, not leaving my hotel room.

# 7

# BELLA

## HER STORY

The day I dreaded came, August 30, 1861. Steven was going away to school. His mother too was leaving on the same train, going back to Pennsylvania to live with her sister. "Just can't work for that woman," she had said about Mrs. Lincoln.

I walked with them to the train. Each of them had one small bag, and I volunteered to carry Mrs. Browning's for her. Soldiers were everywhere, even drilling on the White House lawn.

The train station too was full of soldiers, a sea of blue from their uniforms with some gold mixed in from the braids of the officers. We waited outside. Two army men sat leaning against the wall. One of them, a thin young man with red hair, played a harmonica while his dark-haired friend sang: "Just before the battle, Mother, I am thinking most of you. While upon the field we're waiting with the enemy in view."

Steven's mother shook her head, her eyes closed. "Their poor mothers," she whispered. "I am terrible afraid Joe will be in the war soon."

When they had finished their song, the red-haired man motioned to Steven. "Say, boy, would you like to see how playing a harmonica kept Johnny Reb from killing me?"

"Yes," Steven stepped toward them. The man reached into his pocket and took out another harmonica. A bullet was lodged in it.

"Wow!" said Steven.

Mrs. Browning took his arm. "We'd better get on now," she said. They both turned to look at me.

I looked back, too choked up with tears to speak. "I'll write you letters," Steven said, "and you've got to write back. Tell me what you're doing, and what's going on, you know, at the White House and in the city."

"Good-bye, Bella," said Mrs. Browning, and she hugged me.

They moved away and started up the steps to board the train. Suddenly Steven turned back, jumped from the steps, ran back to me, and kissed me once quickly on the cheek. He whirled to dart toward the train again and bumped into a soldier.

The soldier laughed. "That's right, son," he called to Steven's moving back. "You have to kiss the ladies good-bye, all right."

The men who sat against the wall applauded. Steven found a seat beside a window, but dumbfounded, I could not even wave as the train pulled away.

During the months ahead, I wrote many letters. There was no more school for me, Mistress Newby having turned her building into a hospital, and so I filled my empty days by wandering around Washington City, looking for scenes that might interest Steven.

I wrote about how low wooden hospitals went up on every empty lot, and about how the government Patent Building became a hospital too.

Information about the White House came from my grandmother, who told me about how for a few weeks there were actually soldiers camped on the first floor of the mansion. I wrote too what Grandmother told me about how Mr. Lincoln aged more each day, his face becoming more lined, his bones almost sticking through his skin.

I could not tell Steven about what I actually saw at the White House because I did not go there without him. It had been Steven, so much more than I, who had been friends with the Lincoln boys, Steven who laughed easily when little Tad found and moved the control wheel that made all the bells in the great house sound at once, sending the staff into a state of utter confusion.

It had been Steven who did not hesitate to stop important men and ask, "Please, sir, would you explain what
news there is of the war?" Sometimes he would be brushed
aside, but more often than not something in Steven's
earnest face made the gentleman stop to explain.

From the day when Steven first guided me to the
White House, he had been my passport, the thing that
made me feel my being there was right. After he went
away, I too would have lost contact with the great house
had it not been for Mrs. Keckley, Mrs. Lincoln's dressmaker.

My grandmother came home much excited one day in
October. "Bella," she said even before she had her bonnet
removed. "I've a bit of real news."

I sat at the table reading. My heart skipped forward.
Always, the mention of news made me think of my
father, but Grandmother's news concerned my samplers.
Grandmother had, she informed me, taken them to show
Mrs. Keckley. "'These are remarkable.' That's what she
said, 'remarkable.'" Grandmother dropped the bag containing my samplers on the table. "She wants you to sit in
on the times I help her with Mrs. Lincoln's dresses. She
wants to teach you herself. Can you believe it child, such
a wonderful chance to learn!"

Reluctant to encourage my grandmother further in
her ambitions concerning my becoming a dressmaker, I
voiced the first real worry that came to my mind. "But

Mrs. Lincoln," I protested, "you know how full of moods she is. Won't she rage about me being there?"

Grandmother shook her head. "No, 'tis the strangest thing. Lizzie Keckley seems a pure magician with the woman. I've seen it myself, Mrs. Lincoln in a fit, screaming at us about some little thing. In comes Lizzie, she brushes Mrs. Lincoln's hair or gets her a bouquet of flowers from the conservatory. First thing we know, Mrs. Lincoln is all gentle and sweet." Grandmother took off her bonnet and hung it on the wooden rack beside the door. When she turned back to me, she smiled. "Don't fret over Mrs. Lincoln. She'll be glad enough to have you."

Mrs. Keckley was usually in the White House at least every second day, but the schedule was uncertain. Often Mrs. Lincoln would decide she was wanted for something and send a coach to pick her up. I was to come each afternoon to help in the kitchen unless Mrs. Keckley was present with something she wanted to show me.

I remember so well that first day of instruction. I came to stand in the doorway, hunched and full of dread.

Mrs. Keckley bent over a buttonhole she was making. She wore a black dress with just a slight gathering of white lace at the throat. She was, I knew, in mourning for her son, who had been killed just last month in a battle in Missouri. "Doesn't even have a grave to visit," my grandmother had told me. "He's buried alongside all the others, no names to mark them."

It was my grandmother who noticed me. "Here's Bella," she said.

Mrs. Keckley looked up, her eyes sad but kind. She put down her work, came to take me by the hand, and drew me into the room. "I like teaching girls," she told me. "Been doing so most of my life, slave and free. Last time was in Baltimore where I taught girls of my race to sew. I suspect I still know how to teach." She pulled a chair for me to sit beside her.

After that first lesson, I was never shy with Mrs. Keckley again, and in fact became so comfortable that once when my grandmother was not in the room, I confided in her. I had sat beside her for several lessons by then, and when I conquered a difficult stitch, she said, "You'll be an expert with a needle before you're a woman grown."

I dropped my eyes to study my hands. "Please don't tell my grandmother." I lowered my voice to a whisper. "The truth is, I have no wish to be a dressmaker." I thought suddenly that such a statement might be something of an insult to her and her efforts. "I mean," I added quickly, "it's a fine employment, I'm sure. It must be splendid to make dresses for such grand ladies as Mrs. Lincoln." I shrugged my shoulders. "It is just that since I was but small, I've dreamed of being on the stage."

"Oh, the theater, is it?" She did not speak in such a way as to make me feel ridiculous by indicating her belief that I could never have such a profession. She smiled.

"Well, let's just go on with the lessons, shall we? A body never knows what lies ahead, and dressmaking is a skill that comes in handy in a woman's life. Why, you might want to make costumes for yourself, or for that matter might gain entrance to the theater through making costumes for others."

From that moment on, I became a dedicated student, bringing with me each time a small notebook where I recorded steps just as Mrs. Keckley told them to me. Sometimes, too, I would make simple drawings to help me understand. I was sitting on the back stairs one day waiting for my grandmother and studying my notebook when Willie Lincoln came bounding down the stairs.

He stopped when he saw me. "Bella," he said, and he smiled at me, just a little. He stood beside me, wanting, I thought, to sit down, but like me feeling shy without Steven with us. He paused for a minute, then said, "I've not seen you lately."

"I've been busy," I told him, "learning how to sew from your mother's dressmaker."

Willie smiled again, this time more fully and in a natural way. He moved his hand from the rail and lowered himself to sit beside me. "What's in your notebook?"

I noticed then that he too had a notebook. "Mine has notes from my sewing lesson," I told him. "What's in yours?"

"Mine has my poems in it," he said.

"Poems you liked from your lessons?" I asked.

He shook his head and looked down shyly. "Poems I have written," he said. He studied my face for a minute and decided to risk a question. "Would you like to see the one I'm going to send to the newspaper? It's about the death of Father's friend, Colonel Edward Baker. He got killed in battle."

"I would," I told him. He opened his notebook and pushed it toward me. I do not remember much about the poem, although I was impressed with it. I do remember one line that I read aloud. "His voice is silent in the hall."

"It's because he is dead," Willie explained. "He can't talk anymore. Father cried when he heard the news."

"My father is in the war too," I told him. "I don't live with him, but I got a letter from him yesterday that told me he had joined." I did not tell him that my father fought for the other side.

"How old are you?" he asked.

"Eleven. I just had my birthday."

"I'll be eleven in two months, just before Christmas," he said.

"Steven is twelve. He's gone off to school, you know."

Willie nodded. "We could still be friends, though," he said. "I mean, even without Steven." He laughed a little. "Maybe someday I will write a poem just for you."

"And maybe someday, I will stitch a handkerchief for you."

"Make it blue, if you do," he said. "Blue is my favorite color because it's the color of our uniforms."

Almost every day that fall, Willie would be waiting for me on the stairs after my lesson with Mrs. Keckley. "I watch for you," he told me, "and when I know you are here, I hurry to finish my studies early."

Some days we played marbles. Some days we just talked. Willie told me he worried about his father. "I'm awful afraid someone will hurt him," he said. "Mama says he should be more careful, but he says what will be will be." Willie shrugged. "Sometimes I wish we had never come to Washington City."

"Oh," I said, "but the country needs your father."

He nodded his head and tried to smile. "I know," he said softly. "Besides, if we hadn't come here, I would never have had you for a friend." Walking home that evening, I, too, worried that harm might come to Mr. Lincoln.

"I talk to Willie Lincoln almost every day," I wrote to Steven. "Of course, he could never be my very best friend, like you are, but he is awful nice. He sure does worry about his father."

I had forgotten all about the poem and handkerchief agreement, but Willie hadn't. One cold day in early February he seemed a little quiet when I first joined him. After a few minutes, he said, "I wrote a poem for you, but you might think it is foolish."

"I won't." I shook my head. "I'm sure it is good. Let me see."

"I'll read it," he said, and he took a paper from his pocket.

*When this big house gets sad,*
*Bella makes it not so bad.*
*I always wait for her on the stairs.*
*And when I'm afraid, she cares.*
*She is pretty and very sweet,*
*Being her friend is a real treat.*

Grandmother started down the stairs toward us then. "It's awful nice," I whispered. Embarrassed, I jumped up and hurried toward the backdoor.

"When are you going to make that blue handkerchief for me?" he called after me. Too shy to answer, I just waved my hand at him as I opened the backdoor. The next day Mrs. Keckley told me during my lesson that Willie had developed a fever during the night. "It came on terrible sudden," she said with a sigh. "I'm worried about the child."

A big party had been planned the next day, so there were no lessons. My grandmother, when she finally came home that evening, told me that Willie was worse. "They say he is burning with fever," she said. "Mrs. Lincoln thought to cancel the party, but they decided to go on with it. She was at his bedside often, though, the mister, too. They do dote on that child."

I was sitting beside the fire, but a cold feeling passed through my body. I pulled my shawl closer. "How bad is he?" I asked, and I knew my voice sounded shaky.

My grandmother came over to touch my cheek.

"You've no fever, have you child?" I shook my head. "Don't fret, Bella, girl," she said. "The boy is the son of the president. No expense will be spared. He'll have doctors and medicine aplenty."

I could not eat my supper that night, wanted only to sit beside the fire in an effort to warm away the fear I felt inside. My mother, I was sure, had not wanted for doctors nor for medicine aplenty.

There were no lessons at the White House now. Day after day, Grandmother came home to say Willie had not improved. I wished mightily for blue material to make him a handkerchief. I knew of one piece of blue cloth in the house. In the corner of our tiny cottage sat an old chifforobe that held our meager supply of clothing. Inside, I knew, was my greatest joy, the Sunday dress that my grandmother had recently made for me. It was exactly the right shade of blue. I had worn the dress twice.

Probably if I had told my grandmother how desperately I wanted a piece of bright blue cloth, she would have gotten me one. Never able to talk of the things that meant most to me, I was loath to try to explain. On the fourth day, I could fight the urge no longer. I took the dress from its hanger, caressed the folds of the skirt, carried it to the table, measured, as I had been taught, and cut a large square. I took careful, even stitches to put in the hem. Finishing just before my grandmother was expected, I held it up to admire. Even Mrs. Keckley would say it was well done.

I had no notion of what I would tell my grandmother about the dress or how I would get the gift to Willie. No sewing was being done in the White House. Mrs. Keckley nursed Willie and tried to keep Mrs. Lincoln calm.

When Grandmother did come home that evening, she had news. Tad too was ill. "The little one is no ways as bad as his brother," she said. "Their mother's a wreck, poor thing, but it's Mr. Lincoln as breaks my heart. Oh, the look on that man's face when he comes out of that room." She shook her head. "And him with the weight of this terrible war to boot."

The next day I folded the handkerchief into a small square and put it into my coat pocket. I would, I had decided, take it to the White House. The guard, of course, did not stop me, and I saw no one else as I entered the backdoor and climbed the stairs. On the second floor, the door to Mr. Lincoln's personal office was open. I stopped to look in.

The floor had a dark green carpet. I could see spots of dark green wallpaper too, but mostly the walls were covered with war maps and drawings. Newspapers were stacked on the desk and tables, along with great stacks of mail. Mr. Lincoln sat at the desk, his back to me. He seemed to be staring out the window before him.

I pulled in a great breath and tiptoed into the room to stand beside him. I thought he would turn toward me, but he did not. I waited, but his eyes never left the window. I thought of leaving as quietly as I had come in, but I wanted mightily to give that handkerchief to Willie.

Finally, I put out my hand and touched the top of his long, suit-covered arm. "Mr. President, sir," I whispered softly.

He did not start, did not seem startled at all, but only turned to look at me, a sort of glazed expression in his soft gray eyes. "You're Mistress Cora's granddaughter," he said, and I nodded. "Our Willie's sick, but I suspect you knew that." I nodded again. "Tad too, but the doctor says Tad will mend. Willie, though . . ."

I took the blue material from my pocket, and I held out my hand with it lying flat against my palm. "It's a handkerchief," I said. "I made it special for Willie." Tears were coming up from my chest, and I could hear them in my voice. "He told me he was partial to blue, like the soldiers' uniforms."

"Why, thank you for making it," he said, and taking the handkerchief, he held it up to the light from the window. "You've done fine work. I'll see that Willie gets this."

He laid the cloth on his desk, swiveled in his chair, and put his arms around me. I could feel the sorrow pouring out of his heart, coming through his white shirt and black coat. I could feel the sorrow filling up the room and spilling over into the hall, but when he released me, I looked into his eyes and saw that heartbreak was still there too.

I said nothing more, just turned and moved quickly back into the hall. I never told my grandmother about cutting my Sunday dress. Probably Mrs. Keckley told her about the handkerchief. Maybe she even showed the piece to Grandmother. At any rate, a few days later I was surprised to see that my dress had been remade. The frayed skirt had been removed from the bright blue bodice, and a new skirt of a darker blue attached.

Willie died on February 20. My grandmother came home that evening very tired, her face all drawn with pain. "They say the president said, 'My poor boy. He was too good for this earth, but we loved him so. This is hard, hard.' Then he broke down and cried. I heard him from out in the hall. That great, huge man, broken like a baby." She wiped at her eyes.

The next night after we were in our beds, she asked, "Do you want to see him, child? They've laid him out in the Green Room in a white coffin, and him dressed in a fancy suit. The help all viewed him today, but I can take you tomorrow if you want to go."

I pulled the blanket up to my chin. My first impulse was to say no. I had found no comfort in looking at my mother's white face and closed eyes. I was about to say so when I changed my mind. I could not say why, but I did want to see Willie Lincoln.

My grandmother had said "the green room," and I supposed she meant the president's office, where I had seen the green carpet and green wallpaper. I imagined the white coffin there, surrounded by maps and stacks of newspapers. I wondered if the president would sit at his desk as mourners filed by.

I was wrong. The Green Room was a big parlor on the first floor, with velvet drapes and dark wooden furniture polished to a shine. The coffin stood in the middle of the floor. I dropped Grandmother's hand when we entered the door and moved to stand beside him.

His hair was not wild, as I had always seen it, but neatly combed and parted. His hands were crossed, and he held a bouquet of small purple flowers. I looked down at him and wondered how death could slip into a person and take away the breath. I was ready to step away when I saw the handkerchief. Folded neatly into the breast pocket of his suit jacket was the handkerchief I had made for him. My hand went to my mouth to keep me from crying out loud, but I was glad, deeply glad, I had made the handkerchief.

The rest of that winter was hard for me. Not long after Willie's funeral, Tad did recover, but Mrs. Lincoln, they said, spent most of her days in bed. No parties or dinners were held at the White House, and there was no need for any sewing to be done. Mrs. Keckley spent her days trying to comfort Mrs. Lincoln. I had not supposed I would miss my sewing lessons so much, but I did.

I wrote letters to Steven, and when the winter wind was not sharp, I would walk about Washington City, my head down, thinking of all I had lost, my mother, father,

Steven, and now my new friend Willie. Sometimes I would walk down Pennsylvania Avenue to see the White House in hopes of seeing the president. Poor, dear man, he had loved his son so much. Had my father ever loved me that way? I would stand, staring up at the window where I imagined Mr. Lincoln might sit, and I would pretend that he was my father. It was all right, I told myself, to pretend. After all, I did not even know where my own father was.

# 8

# WILKES

HIS STORY

———◆———

I cannot understand Lucy. She is like no other woman I have ever known. Always I have been able to lead women to think as I think. Yet here is a woman who loves me, I know she does. Still she will not agree with me about the Union or about the evils of Abraham Lincoln.

"You could not say he is heartless had you attended his son's funeral," she told me at dinner one evening. "The sorrow in that man's face." She closed her eyes for a moment and shook her head slightly.

I reached across the table to take her hand. "Do not waste your sympathy, my darling," I said. "I've no doubt the man appeared sorry. I've never said he was a fool, but let me assure you his heart is too hard to be touched by the death of a mere child."

"No," she protested, her voice strong. "I know Robert Lincoln. He was shaken by his brother's death, and told me that his father would never be the same."

I saw a way out of the discussion. Any talk of Lincoln in real human terms distressed me. "You know Robert Lincoln?" We had never talked of young Lincoln, and I had never told her that it was seeing her with the man that had first sparked my interest in her. The idea would have made her angry. I adopted a teasing tone. "How well do you know the president's son?"

Lucy smiled. "He was my escort on several occasions, nothing more."

"Ah," I said, remembering how young Lincoln looked at her, "I'd wager there was something more on his part."

Lucy shrugged. "Perhaps for a time, but I could never be interested in him. He looks more like his mother than his father."

I laughed. "Don't tell me you would ever have been seen in public with him if he looked like his father!"

Lucy raised her eyebrows. "Looks, Wilkes, are not everything, and yes, had I seen anything of the father in Robert Lincoln, you might have had a harder time winning my affection."

How could I disagree? Had I not thought Lucy plain that first night? Now I found her wildly attractive, more pleasing than all the other women in my life. "Marry me, Lucy," I said. "Marry me now, no matter what your father thinks."

"I cannot marry you now, Wilkes, and my father is only one reason." She slipped a ring from her finger and put it on my smallest finger. "Wear this ring to remind you of me. I have not told you yet, but Father has been appointed the ambassador to Spain. We leave in the spring. I will stay there one year, and if during all that time you have been faithful only to me, I will return and marry you no matter what my father says."

I was too overcome to speak. I lifted my hand, kissed the ring. Next I lifted her hand and pressed it to my lips. We were engaged! Of course we were not able to make the fact public knowledge, but I knew, and my heart almost burst with joy.

My personal happiness, though, could not outweigh my distress over what was happening to the South and over Lincoln's reelection. No president in my lifetime had been elected to a second term. "He will make himself king now," I told Asia. My sister would listen to my concerns, even though she did not believe in the Southern cause.

We were in her home in Philadelphia, where I had gone to star in a play. Asia had made a small supper for me, and her husband playing out of town gave us a chance to talk. "I feel I should do something," I told her. "I really do."

Asia got up from her chair and came to stand beside mine. She put her arm around my shoulders and leaned her head down to rest on mine. "Don't fret so, Wilkes. I worry about you. Sometimes you seem to worry almost to the point of breaking. 'Let us be happy.' Remember that is what you told me once. You have such a fire, my sweet boy. Don't let this war burn you out."

I tried to heed my sister's words. I even agreed to perform with my brothers. My mother was pleased. At last she had the chance to see her three actor sons on the stage together. June came in from California, and it was arranged that he, Edwin, and I should appear together in New York in a benefit performance to raise money for a wonderful bronze statue of William Shakespeare to be placed in Central Park.

I did not like the idea. Edwin actually supported Lincoln, admitted out loud that he voted for the man, and wanted to hear nothing of my love for the South. We were sitting in the living room of his New York home. I jumped to my feet. "You've turned your back on our home. You've betrayed Maryland," I accused him.

"Maryland did not secede," he answered calmly.

The ease of his manner infuriated me! Could he not see that the matter we discussed was important, was everything? "We should have seceded, by thunder! Look how Lincoln treats us, guarding our borders with suspicion and taking away our writ of habeas corpus, locking people up at will!"

He yawned! Yes, I tell you, he yawned. "How can a man as intelligent as you, Wilkes, not see that the Union must be preserved?" He picked up a book as if to show me the discussion was at an end. "Your beloved South cannot stand. You may as well get used to the idea."

I walked out of his house then, and I decided that I would not go back except to see Mother, who is often there caring for Edwin's motherless daughter. I hate being at odds with Edwin. Nothing else has ever divided us. People suppose that there is professional jealousy between us, both of us prominent actors. Ah, yes, there is talk. . . . Who is the greatest Booth? Which brother is the country's leading actor? We pay them no heed. We are brothers. When I followed Edwin to the stage, he found true delight in my success in what is, after all, the family business.

Well, why should the Booth boys be any different from the countless other brothers this war has divided? It is, indeed, "A War of Brothers." June and Joseph support Lincoln too. My brothers' desertion of me prompted my selection of the quote I had printed on show cards and playbills. It is a quote from Richard in *Richard III*: "I have no brother, I am no brother . . . I AM MYSELF ALONE."

June is kinder to me on the subject. He was away from the family for so many years managing theaters and doing some acting out west. "This is all a family quarrel, a big family quarrel, I'll admit, but a family fuss still. It will pass, just as your hard feelings toward Edwin will pass."

Had it not been for June, acting as peacemaker, Edwin and I would never have been able to perform together.

The play was Shakespeare's *Julius Caesar*, one of the few pieces with three strong leads for men. Edwin was Brutus, June played Cassius, and I was Marc Antony.

It was late November and bitter cold in New York. Lincoln had been reelected, and my spirits were low. The play was held at the Winter Garden, a lovely old Broadway playhouse named for one in Paris. Mother sat in a box just above the stage, and she was radiant in a black dress with a white collar. On her face was a look of complete happiness. Dear Mother! I loved my mother, hated to grieve her.

The house was packed. The Booth boys raised $3,500 for the statue! There was a party at Edwin's after the play, everyone laughing and dancing. I pretended to smile, but the air seemed stale to me. I had to loosen my collar in order to breathe freely.

Then I heard Edwin. He was talking, surrounded by people, but Edwin's voice, of course, carries. I heard every word. I stood slightly away from the crowd, leaning against a doorframe. Edwin spoke of being at a dinner party with Abraham Lincoln, spoke of it with pride! The party was at the home of William H. Seward, secretary of state, a man I hate almost as much as I hate Lincoln.

Edwin told how Mr. Seward and Mr. Lincoln had gone several times to see him in plays at the National Theatre in Washington City, and Edwin felt honored. "What an exhilarating experience! Sitting at the same dinner table with Abraham Lincoln! Seward's daughter was wild to have my autograph, but I tell you it felt strange for me to be the one signing autographs in the presence of such greatness!"

I left the party then. Found Mother, kissed her quickly, and made for the door, almost unable to breathe. At first I took a hansom cab, but then I got out to walk. The wind was sharp, but I seemed to feel no cold except the cold that came from inside me. I walked along the water, stared out at the dark waves, and searched for answers.

Over the sound of the ocean, I began to recite the speech from the play I had just performed, the words that announced the death of Caesar:

> *"Liberty! Freedom! Tyranny is dead!*
> *Run hence, proclaim, cry it about the streets."*

I wondered why the words resounded so in my memory. They certainly did not apply to my life. Tyranny was not dead in America, where a tyrant had just been elected for a second term. I began to shake uncontrollably, and yet I was perspiring too. I thought bright orange lights came from the ocean.

Finally my head cleared. I hailed a cab, went to the train station, and caught a train back to Washington City.

# 9

# ARABELLA

HER STORY

———◆———

The winter of Willie's death passed. I went back to the White House, working in the kitchen and picking up my lessons. For two years I studied dressmaking with Mrs. Keckley, and for two years I listened and watched for news of the war. How torn I was, a girl who worked in the White House and who admired Mr. Lincoln beyond my weak ability to express, yet whose heart remembered tenderly her old life in Richmond and the long-ago father who now wore the uniform of gray.

I discussed the torment caused by my divided loyalties only with Steven. During those many hours of letter writing, I had discovered that the tongue-tied girl of my childhood could, with a pen in hand, express herself well. And so our letters became the foundation for our always deepening friendship, one between two young people who knew and understood each other profoundly.

I wrote to Steven about how Union victories in the South had brought former slaves to Washington City by the thousands, carrying with them almost nothing. They were called contrabands because they were considered to be property seized during war.

They lived in camps set up by the government down by the soggy, stinking Washington Canal, entire families huddled beneath a makeshift shanty roof that did not even keep the rain out. They were hungry and often cold and sick. Mrs. Keckley worked long hours speaking in various churches to raise money to help them, and she worked in the camps with other women to teach the children to read and to encourage the adults to plant vegetable gardens.

"Weren't they better off as slaves?" I asked her once as she told me about the terrible conditions under which the people lived.

We were sitting at a table, sewing, and she leaned toward me. "Oh, no, Bella, never. We have to think of the future, of the next generation. The first steps to freedom may be very hard, but those steps must be made! It is better to starve as a free man than to eat well as a slave."

On January 1, 1863, the president had signed the Emancipation Proclamation, which said that all slaves in states in rebellion against the Union were officially free. Of course, as Steven pointed out to me, the Confederacy paid no attention and freed no slaves, and the proclamation did not free the slaves in the border states where some people still owned them.

Before the Emancipation Proclamation, the war had been about secession, not slavery, but the proclamation settled for all time the fate of slavery in America. If the Union won the war, slavery everywhere would end. The proclamation also stated that men of color could now be used in the Union Army and Navy.

Steven and I discussed all of that in our letters. He sent me a tintype of himself in his school uniform. He had grown taller, and there was a serious look in his blue eyes. We had not seen each other in three years, and to help me feel closer to him, I frequently leaned the picture against a pitcher that stood on the table where I wrote letters.

I told Steven of my changing attitude toward Mrs. Lincoln. "Yes, she can be difficult," I wrote, "but I've come to appreciate some things about her, for instance, the way she works in the hospitals caring for the wounded. It has helped her deal with her grief over Willie."

In the fall of 1863 a letter had come from my aunt in Richmond. This one was addressed to me. "Dear Bella," it said, "I am sending this letter with a friend of mine who will be traveling North. I do hope it reaches you." I looked up in the right-hand corner and noticed that the date of the letter was in August. I read on, "Your father was in the Battle of Gettysburg. We know for sure that he was not injured, but he was taken prisoner. We heard from a man who was with him that most of the prisoners from that battle went to Fort Delaware. There has been no word directly from your father. I imagine that you consider yourself a Northerner now, but still, surely you can find it in your heart to pray for one Southern prisoner."

I put down the letter to wipe the tears from my eyes. "The Battle of Gettysburg," I whispered to myself. It had happened in July. I remembered what I had heard at the White House, where I now spent most of my days. General Lee's army had moved up the Shenandoah Valley into Pennsylvania. They had planned to destroy railroads and move on, maybe even all the way to Washington City to take the Union's capital.

The battle had raged on for three days, dead men on both sides everywhere. Finally the Confederate forces were beaten into retreat. There was much celebration in the White House. It was, they said, the turning point of the war.

I had been there outside the president's personal office. I heard the talk, and I had rejoiced with them when the South was defeated. After all, I did not want the enemy army in Washington City. I did not suppose that harm would come to me, but I knew the Lincolns would be in danger, and I feared for Mrs. Keckley. I did not think the Southern army would be kind to a former slave who was now the best friend of the president's wife.

Holding my aunt's letter, I looked back on those days. I had not been thinking about my own father when I prayed that the Southern army would be defeated. Now I felt even more torn between the two sides.

In the fall of 1864, my grandmother became ill with a fever. After a few days, the fever subsided, but Grandmother's strength never returned. At the same time her rheumatism grew worse, leaving her fingers terribly twisted.

Mrs. Keckley assured me I was ready to take Grandmother's place. "She's as good as her grandmother now, and she will be far superior with a bit more practice," I heard her say to Mrs. Lincoln, and I appreciated the way I was welcomed warmly as a full-time White House worker.

One November afternoon a knock sounded on the sewing room door. I put down my work and moved to answer. It took an instant for me to realize that the young man who stood outside the door in a blue uniform was really Steven. A scream of joy escaped from my lips, and I put my hands over my mouth. He picked me up, and laughing and crying at once, I hugged him.

He was, he told me, in Washington City, only for one day and night, having secured a ride with a teacher who drove his coach to Washington City on business. There was to be a huge party at the White House that evening. I was afraid I might be needed to help with preparations, but Mrs. Keckley was in the room and witnessed our joyful reunion.

"Go," she said. "Go and have a good time."

And go we did, laughing down the hall. On the stairs,

I stopped for a moment and squeezed Steven's arm. "I remember the day you first led me up these steps," I said, looking up at him. "You were much shorter then."

"You've changed too." He grinned. "You were pretty then. Now you're beautiful." For an instant, something in his voice and in the way he looked at me made me self-conscious, but the feeling passed quickly. I had my dear old friend back with me for a few hours, and it felt so good.

Although it was almost winter, the day was not bitterly cold as it had been the day before. At the first street corner, the smell of roasting chestnuts filled the air. "Are you hungry?" Steven asked.

"We can have our supper with Grandmother, " I said. "I made a big soup."

Steven laughed. "I didn't travel to Washington City to be poisoned by your cooking. We'll buy something to eat for supper, but first we'll have chestnuts."

"The money," I protested, but Steven shook his head.

"I've been given an increase in my allowance from the trust fund, and I've saved for just such a day. I plan to come to see you in August too, before I go to Harvard." He smiled at me. "We've been too long apart, Bella." We moved to the little brown cart. The vendor bent over his wares, and his brown coat and hat made him seem to be an extension of the contraption. "Give us four," said Steven, and he handed money to the man, who raised his head to smile at us.

"You've a pretty lady by your side, son," said the man

as he handed us our bag, "'Tis a fine thing to be young and walk out with a pretty lady."

"It is," said Steven. I blushed and thought I should explain to the man that Steven and I were not actually "walking out together," that we were not sweethearts, just old friends reunited for the day, but Steven took my hand and led me away.

He was interested in our streetcars that glided down rails and were pulled by big, powerful horses. Although the streetcars were two years old in our city, I had never ridden one. I could easily walk to the White House from my home, and every penny was needed for necessities.

Of course, Steven insisted we ride. The seats were enclosed, but above them the cars were open. Even though the day was not bitter, the streetcar moved fast enough to create a sharp breeze that stung at my cheeks, and I buried my face in the arm of Steven's coat. I felt happy there, taking in the smell of the wool material mixed with the familiar scent of his skin, and I reluctantly moved my head to eat the chestnut he urged me to take.

Near Maryland Avenue, we got off the streetcar to walk. An old brick building there had been built to serve as a temporary capitol when the real capitol was burned during the War of 1812. When I first came to Washington City, the building had contained a school, but now it was used as a prison for Southern soldiers.

We stopped to watch a group of guards move new prisoners into the building. The Southern men were connected to each other by chains fastened around their ankles.

One man, who seemed old for a soldier, turned and met my gaze. His eyes were blue and full of sadness. I had to turn away and did not watch as they moved slowly into the prison. "I wish my father could be in this one," I said. "Perhaps they would let me in to see him."

"This war will surely be over soon," said Steven. "You can see your father then."

We made our supper of oysters and hot buns we bought from a vendor. As we pulled the bits of meat from the shell with our fingers, Steven talked about Harvard. "Remember, it's where Robert Lincoln went," he said.

I nodded. "He's in the army now," I said, but I was not thinking much about Robert. "Massachusetts is even farther away from here than Pennsylvania is." I studied the oyster shell I held in my hand.

Steven reached out to take my hand, closing my fingers around the shell. "We can write letters," he said. "You write wonderful letters, Bella," but his words did not ease the pain I felt inside when I thought about Steven leaving me again.

After the meal, we walked about Washington City, commenting on the sights as we had done as children. On Tenth Street, we saw people going into Ford's Theatre. "Would you like to see a play?" Steven asked.

All day I had been hesitant to have him spend his money on me, but now I nodded quickly. We moved through the crowd of people in evening clothes to the ticket window. "Sorry," said the man when we asked for tickets. "There aren't any for tonight's performance. You've got to get here early when J. Wilkes Booth is starring."

We turned away to look at the advertisements. I pointed to a likeness of Mr. Booth. "I saw him when I was with my mother in Richmond," I said. "We were going into the theater just as he was. He held the door for us." I smiled, remembering. "He looked down at me and smiled. It wasn't long before my mother died. I was only eight years old, but I never forgot him, his unusual eyes. He was not the star of the play that day, but when he came on-stage, my mother whispered his name to me. I've always wanted to see him again."

"Wait here," said Steven, and he went back to the ticket window. When he came back, he handed me a ticket. "It's for tomorrow evening," he said.

Tears of joy came to my eyes as I thanked him. "You are the dearest friend I could ever have," I said.

We stayed for a while, looking at the show cards that advertised plays and watching the people going inside. "Remember what Mrs. Keckley told you about working in a costume shop?" Steven said. "Maybe it is time for you to try your hand at that."

We had stepped away by then, and I turned to look back at the big building, three stories high. Could I work there? Could I be part of Ford's Theatre? A thrill went through my body. "You give me courage," I said. "I'll go there day after tomorrow and ask for a part-time job. I think seeing a show first will make me braver."

Steven wanted a look at the White House all lit up at night, so we rode the streetcar back there. The party had started. We stood on the north lawn admiring the lights and listening to the bits of music that drifted to our ears. "It still seems like home to me," said Steven. "The guards all know you, don't they? Let's go inside."

As it turned out, the guard was a young man Steven had known when his mother worked there. "I've done been in the war and back," said James when Steven told him who he was. "Does it last much longer, you'll be trading that school uniform for a fighting one."

"It won't last that long," I said, and I pulled Steven away from the war talk. Inside, we went to a back hall. "I'd best stay out of sight," I said. "If Mrs. Lincoln sees me, she's likely to put me to work."

We could hear the music well, and I began to sway with it. "Let's dance," Steven said.

I felt suddenly very shy. "I can't dance," I said, looking down. "I've never learned."

"It isn't so hard," he said. "Just follow me." Steven reached to pull me into his arms. For a minute we moved to the music, but then I stepped on his foot. We both stumbled and laughed.

"That's enough," I said, pulling away from his arms. Steven held tight to my hand.

"You said something earlier that I didn't like." His face was suddenly very serious.

I strained, trying to remember anything I might have said that would disturb him, but he went on. "You said I was the dearest friend you could ever have."

"You are," I said.

Steven shook his head. "But you see that's what I didn't like. I don't want to be your friend anymore," he said. "Well, not just your friend. I want to be more to you than a friend, Bella."

My knees felt weak, and I leaned against the wall. Steven dropped my hand and came to me. Putting his hand beneath my chin, he kissed me lightly on the lips. "Someday I mean to marry you, Bella Getchel," he said. He took my hand and led me back outside. Neither of us said anything until we were outside.

"I'd better go home," I said then. "My grandmother will be worried about me if I stay much later."

"I'll walk with you," he said. On the way home we talked of ordinary things, his school, my work at the White House, but his words were between us. We could both feel them. Outside my door, we said good-bye, me wiping away tears.

"Don't cry, Bella," he said. "Don't cry, and don't forget what I said." He touched my cheek. Then he was gone. I stood watching him until he disappeared into the night.

I thought of Steven all the next day as I sewed. "Did you have a good time with your young man?" Mrs.

Keckley asked, and I told her I had. I did not even protest that Steven was not my young man.

That evening I went inside Ford's Theatre for the first time. My seat was near the front, and I could see Mr. Booth plainly. A chill went through me each time he spoke. What a thrill it would be, I thought, to work in the same building with him. If I were to get work in the costume shop, I would be bound to see him, wouldn't I? I might even have a chance to actually talk to him.

The next day I went back to the theater. For a long time I stood beneath one of the rounded archways and tried to get up my courage. I pictured Steven's face, and I imagined I could hear him say, "Go on in, Bella. You won't get a job standing out here."

Finally I did go inside and was directed to the costume shop. The costume mistress insisted I call her Lillie. "Everyone does round here, young and old," she said.

I felt comfortable with Miss Lillie at once. When she told me that there was no position open for a paid seamstress, I suggested that perhaps I could work a few hours each week in exchange for tickets.

And so, I was sewing at Ford's Theatre in December of 1864 when I first saw Wilkes Booth, when he came into the costume shop of Ford's Theatre with the lady and told the story of his parents' meeting.

It was only my second time there. I threaded a needle, and then, still holding the needle in the air, I asked, "Does Mr. Booth come into the shop often?"

Lillie laughed. "Wanting to see Wilkes Booth, are you? Well, everyone does." She put down her work, yawned, and stretched. "Yes, I expect you'll see him come in the door any minute." She lifted the costume again. "This here's his coat, and he likes to check on his things."

"Is he married?" I asked.

Lillie laughed again. "No, I can't imagine the man with a wife, though some say he's engaged secretly to a young woman named Lucy, some senator's daughter. If it's true, it doesn't seem to have slowed him down much with other ladies."

It was not fifteen minutes later when Mr. Booth came in with a lady I heard him call Martha. She had asked, just as they came in, how his parents had met. He told the story then about his mother being a flower girl. We all listened. After the story of the meeting was over, the lady whispered something into his ear.

I thought it rude of her to whisper with other people in the room. Mr. Booth did not seem to think her rude, however, and he laughed when she tossed her head and left the room. I had no idea what she said, but the way Wilkes looked at her was enough to make my face turn red.

He noticed me then. I could feel his eyes on my burning face, but I looked only at the hem of the coat I held in my lap. My heart pounded as I heard his steps on the floor. "Lillie," he said to the costume mistress, "who is this beauty, and how long have you hidden her away in this dreary shop?"

Mistress Lillie was a kind woman. Her mouth was full of pins, but she removed them. "Stop where you are, Wilkes. This shop is my domain, and I won't have you dallying with Bella right before my eyes, her a girl of only fourteen."

He stopped, put up his hands as if to surrender. "Fourteen?" he said. "I thought her much older. I would never, as you say, 'dally' with a girl so young." He laughed. "I think, though, that I might be allowed to speak to her." He moved closer to me. "You aren't afraid of me, are you—" He paused. "Bella, is it?"

I do not know what made me answer him as I did, but I looked up at him and said, "My full name is Arabella." It was a fact I had never mentioned to anyone else in Washington City.

He cocked his head, and his dark eyes studied me a moment. "Arabella," he repeated my name slowly. "It suits you better than Bella. Arabella is a beautiful name for a beautiful young lady. I am Wilkes Booth." He held out his hand, and I placed my fingers across his palm. He bowed and kissed my hand. "You did not answer my question. Are you afraid of me, Arabella?"

I had to look slightly away from those eyes before I could speak. "No, sir," I said, "I am not afraid of you." It was a lie. I did fear him, feared the weak feeling I had when his eyes looked deep into mine.

"How do you come to be here in the costume shop?" he asked. "A girl with your beauty is more often found on the stage."

"I sew for tickets." I hesitated, looking down again at my sewing, then went on, "I love the theater."

"Do you, Arabella?"

"Yes, my mother used to take me to the theater in Richmond. In fact, I saw you once there. You held the door for us, and then I saw you on the stage."

"Richmond!" His face lit up as if a spotlight had been turned on it. "Are you from Richmond?" I looked about suddenly and realized that Mistress Lillie and the other woman had left the room. I was alone with this man!

"Yes, sir," I said. "I lived there with my mother and father until my mother died. Now I live with my grand-mother here in Washington City."

"So you are a Virginia girl. I can't believe I could have forgotten meeting you, but then, you must have been a child at the time." He nodded his head, "A Virginia girl," he said again. "Little wonder then that I find myself so drawn to you. I spent many good days in Richmond. Why do you not live with your father in Richmond now?"

I could not say to him, could I, that my father did not want me, had not wanted me for these past six years. Instead I said, "My father is a prisoner of war."

"Ah." His face grew sad. "I am sorry if my inquiry caused you pain." He lowered his voice. "It must be hard for you, a daughter of the South, in this city."

I wanted to tell him that I didn't actually consider my-self a daughter of the South anymore, that I loved Mr.

Lincoln and believed in the Union, but I didn't. The light that came to his eyes left me with no doubt that he was a Copperhead, a Southern sympathizer in the North, and so great was his charm, so handsome was his face, that I felt unable to disagree with him.

I ignored his comment about the South and said, "I've always dreamed of being on the stage."

"Have you now?" He smiled at me, reached into his pocket, and took out a folded piece of paper. "Would you like to learn some lines of poetry?" he asked. "You could say them for me as a sort of audition."

The wave of excitement that passed through me threatened to take my breath away, but I managed to say, "Yes! Oh, yes, sir. I would love to do that." I held out my shaking hand for the paper.

"It's by Edgar Allan Poe," he said, and he began to recite the poem, "It was many and many a year ago, In a kingdom by the sea, That a maiden there lived whom you may know, By the name of Annabel Lee." He stopped. "Well, enough of me. You learn it and say it for me." He cocked his head, studying me. "Yes, I should enjoy hearing you, I'm sure."

"Oh, thank you, sir."

He turned and walked toward the door. Just before he went out, he looked back at me. "There is one more thing I must ask of you, Arabella."

"Yes, sir." I waited.

He laughed. "Will you please stop calling me sir?

You make me feel old, practically ancient, instead of twenty-six."

I put down my sewing and read the poem over and over. By the time I walked home that evening, I had memorized most of the lines.

That night I wrote a long letter to Steven. "Things are beginning to happen, just as you said they might. I've had a chance to talk to the actor I told you about, Wilkes Booth," I told him. "He gave me a piece to memorize, said he wants to hear me recite. Could this be the beginning of my life on the stage? Thank you, dear Steven, for encouraging me to go to Ford's for work. I would never have done it without your urging."

For the first time, I held back a true emotion, did not tell Steven how Wilkes Booth made me feel. Nor did I tell Steven that I had let the man believe I was a Copperhead. Steven, I knew, would tell me to steer clear of Wilkes. Steven would see that I might be headed for danger. I did not want to hear such words because I knew I would not heed them.

I spent days practicing the short piece. I wished I could do it before the small mirror above our washstand, but Grandmother was always in the house, and she would have questioned me about the activity. I had upset Grandmother enough by insisting that I sew for theater tickets.

"No good will come of this hanging around show

people." She made a small clucking sound with her tongue. "But now that you're the one who supports me instead of the other way around, I suppose there is little hope that you will listen to me." She peered up at from where she sat, and I softened at the true concern I saw there on her old face.

"I do listen to you, Grandmother." I bent to her rocker before the fire, and I kissed her cheek. "I do listen to you, dear one, but I also listen to my heart. My heart tells me to work in the theater, but I will be careful."

I was not careful about Wilkes Booth. Our second meeting was on the streets of Washington City. It was early on a cold day in February. I had pulled my shawl up over my head as I hurried toward my job at the White House.

A hansom cab passed me and stopped. From the carriage Wilkes Booth called, "Arabella, is that you?"

Dumbfounded that he should recognize me, I stood for a second unable to speak. Then I found my voice. "Yes," I cried into the wind.

He motioned with his arm that I should come to him. "I'll give you a ride in my cab," he said. "You must be half frozen."

I ran toward him. Wilkes Booth had recognized me on the street and offered me a ride. This was the most exciting thing that had ever happened to me. Mistress Lillie's words to him about dallying with me flashed through my mind, but I did not slow my step. He would never make improper gestures toward me. Of that fact I felt certain, and I must say that he never did. He never made unseemly remarks or tried to touch me in an indecent way.

As graceful as a cat, he jumped from the carriage to take my arm and help me climb inside. "Where are you going so early?" he asked when he was settled in beside me.

"To the White House," I said. "I am assistant to Mrs. Lincoln's dressmaker."

I thought he might ask me to get out, might not want to carry an employee of the White House in his cab, but he did not. "Pennsylvania Avenue, Zeke," he called to the driver who sat above the carriage. "We've an employee of the president here."

We had traveled just half a block when the carriage slowed at the corner. Wilkes took off his large top hat and tipped it to a lady standing on the steps of her boarding-house. He leaned out and called, "Good morning, Mrs. Surratt."

I knew the woman because my grandmother had done some sewing for her and her daughter Anna, who was a pretty young woman. I wondered if Wilkes knew Mrs. Surratt because he had stepped out with Anna.

He was dressed as for evening in a dark suit with tails, a sparkling white shirt, and a tall silk hat. He had been, I supposed, at a party all night, and was only now going home.

Someone had doubtless danced with him. An image flashed through my mind. I saw myself, dressed in a delightful green dress. I was moving about the floor in the arms of Wilkes Booth. I shook my head ever so slightly to clear my mind.

"Tell me," he said, "how do you like working for the mighty Lincolns?" A sneer moved across his lips as he said the words.

I looked down at the hands I twisted in my lap. "Don't mind me," he said, his voice and expression kind again. "I hate the tyrant, but I will not blame you if you don't."

"They have been naught but kind to me," I said, my eyes still down.

"And does this kind Lincoln know your father fought for the South?"

"He does," I said. I remembered the day I told Mr. Lincoln about my father. It was soon after the letter from my aunt arrived. "What's wrong with our Bella?" the president asked me one day. He had come upon me crying as I sewed. My sad tale came tumbling out.

"I am sorry to hear of your troubles, Miss Bella, most sorely sorry." He had bent to pat my hand. "The sorrow over this war mounts higher than all the mountains of this nation, north and south."

Now I cleared my throat, and looking away from Wilkes to gaze out the window of the carriage, I found courage to say, "Mr. Lincoln offered his sympathy to me, said he was sorry for my troubles."

"And well he should be sorry, sorry indeed. Did you know that he has stopped the prisoner exchange?"

"I am not sure what the prisoner exchange is," I said. I gave a little shrug of my shoulders. "I am afraid I am not always clear about what's happening with the war. My friend Steven is better at it all."

"Lincoln has stopped exchanging Union prisoners for Confederate prisoners." The snarl returned to his face. "You see, that was the practice for some time, but Lincoln decided it would hurt the Southern war effort if the exchange stopped. There are more soldiers in the North, especially now that he uses the colored men. They do not need returned soldiers to go back to battle nearly as badly as the South needs her men."

"Oh," I said softly.

"Yes, your father and thirty-five thousand other Southern men will now sit in prison for the duration of this war. You can thank your Mr. Lincoln for that!" He turned away from me for a moment toward the window. When he looked at me again, he smiled. "But let us not talk of dreary things. Tell me, have you learned the lines I gave you?"

"I have," I said.

He leaned back on the seat and folded his arms across his chest. "Well, Miss Arabella, will you do me the honor of reciting for me?"

My heart pounded, but I drew a deep breath. "'Annabel Lee' by Edgar Allan Poe," I said.

"Look at me as you speak," said Wilkes.

I did and felt a great surge of energy. I recited clearly and in a good strong voice, putting in every drop of emotion inside me.

"Bravo," Wilkes said when I finished, and he clapped his hands. "Next time we shall take you up to the stage and let the company manager hear you too. I'll find you in the costume shop when there is a good chance."

"Oh, thank you, sir," I said, and a great wave of happiness rushed through my body.

"Now," he said, "tell me about this Steven. Is he your beau?"

"Until recently I had never thought of Steven in that way, but now I think perhaps he is." I laughed. "I only know I cannot imagine life without him. He is my best and dearest friend." I paused. "And yes, perhaps, my beau."

Wilkes looked at me, his eyes boring into my very being. "He is a lucky young man, to be the dearest friend of the beautiful Arabella who is, I am certain, as beautiful as the beautiful Annabel Lee."

The cab came to a stop then in front of the White House. Wilkes jumped out to help me alight. "Thank you, sir," I said again. "Thank you for the ride and for all your kind help."

He bowed to me. "Good-bye, Miss Arabella." He was about to climb back into the cab when he looked back at

me. "Arabella," he said with a laugh. "I've asked you before not to call me sir."

"I won't, s——" I almost said *sir,* and we both laughed.

"Can't you say Wilkes?" he called from the cab.

"Good-bye, Wilkes," I shouted. I watched the hansom cab disappear, and I felt good, wonderfully good.

# 10

# WILKES

### HIS STORY

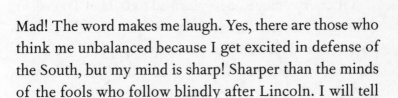

Mad! The word makes me laugh. Yes, there are those who think me unbalanced because I get excited in defense of the South, but my mind is sharp! Sharper than the minds of the fools who follow blindly after Lincoln. I will tell you how keen is my thinking!

I watched the girl go into the White House, and the idea came to me. One moment I was staring at her back, wondering how sweet, charming Arabella could bear to work in the house of the devil himself, and the next moment the idea had sprung full-blown from my brain, as Athena sprang full-blown from the head of Zeus. So filled with excitement was I that I pounded my walking stick against the top of the carriage and shouted, "I am a genius!"

The driver drew the horses to a stop. He leaned down toward my window and shouted, "Is something wanted, sir?"

"Oh, no," I called. "Sorry to have interrupted, Zeke."

"At your service, sir," he said.

I decided to give Zeke an even larger tip than usual, and I will remember that his cab was the lucky one where the wonderful idea came to me. I leaned back against the seat and thought about being a genius.

My father was a genius. Everyone said so. He was the finest actor ever to appear on the American stage. So great was he that when he died one theater critic wrote, "There are no more actors."

Of course, they said he was mad too. "Mad Tragedian Returns to Boston Stage." So read the headlines in a Boston newspaper. Edwin showed the paper to Asia and me after he returned from a tour with Father. Edwin waited until Joseph, two years younger than I, was not about, then he called Asia and me into his room.

Edwin traveled with Father as had our brother June before him. They were there to help with his costume changes, to keep track of stage props, and to do such jobs as dab him, between scenes, with the red makeup that looked like blood. They were also supposed to keep him from drinking and, I learned that day, to follow after him in an effort to protect him when madness settled over him.

"It's true," Edwin said after Asia and I had read the headlines. "Our father is mad, and you may as well know it now." He took the newspaper from my hands, folded it, and put it in his bureau drawer.

"Why would you want to keep such a thing?" I asked. "I do not believe those words, and neither should you."

Edwin whirled back to me, agitated. "You do not have to see him when the madness comes. You are safe at home while I have to run after him. Last week in Boston, he gave them a show." Edwin waved his arms. "No, not on the stage, and don't say alcohol caused it. He was stone sober. Yet he bought a delivery wagon full of flour, paid the driver twice its worth, then hacked open the kegs and drove down the streets with a white cloud drifting after him."

Edwin walked back and forth, words rolling from his mouth. "Once he paid a hearse to carry a bunch of dead pigeons to a cemetery, where he had them buried. He even tried to pay a minister to do a service. The man is mad, and we who are of his blood are likely to follow after him."

"He is kindhearted," I protested. "You know how he won't allow us to kill even an insect." I looked at Asia for support, but she shook her head.

"I am afraid Edwin is right about Father," she said. "June told Mother stories of strange actions too. I sometimes hid from sight and listened."

Our brother June, whose real name is Junius Brutus Booth the second, is seventeen years older than I am. He traveled with Father when I was very young. I could not believe that Asia, who usually told me everything, had kept a secret from me for so long.

"You did not tell me," I said, and miserable, I moved away from them to stand beside the window and stare out at the sycamore tree.

"I did not wish to worry you," she said.

"There is no denying Rosalie has an odd turn," I said. Our sister, just younger than June, had never made friends and stayed home, mostly in her room. "And even Joseph suffers from long periods of melancholia. Are we all destined for insanity?" Tears rolled down my cheeks.

"See what you have caused, Edwin!" Asia came to me and touched my arm. "We are fine, Johnny. There is no sign of Father's pain in the three of us." She waved her hand to include Edwin. "Don't fret. You are like Father, but not in that way. You have his fire, the spirit that draws people to you, but you do not have his demons." She hugged me. "I am sure of that."

We were young then, I around twelve, Asia three years older, and Edwin two years older than she. Sitting in Zeke's hansom cab, I wondered if Asia would still argue that I do not have Father's malady. Oh, yes, I think she would, even if she knew my plan.

Edwin thinks me mad. He said as much when last I saw him. I had gone to his home to visit Mother, thinking Edwin was touring. He was there, though, and he followed me to the door when I left. After I said good-bye to

Mother, he stepped outside and closed the door behind him.

"Wilkes," he said, "I ran into John Ford at a party a few nights ago. He told me you were spewing political nonsense all over Washington City."

I had started down the steps, but I whirled back. For one moment I considered hitting Edwin, knocking him down the steps, but I remembered our mother was in the house. I took a deep breath and pushed my rage down inside. "I've never made an effort to hide my views from John Ford or anyone else."

"Mark my words," said Edwin, and he actually shook his finger at me. "You can go too far with your Southern nonsense, even if you are a Booth. How would it make you feel if John Ford decided not to let you appear in his theater?"

I shoved my hands into my pocket to keep from using them on my brother. "What do I care for appearing in Ford's theater or any other playhouse?" I gritted my teeth and then went on. "Listen to me, Edwin. I intend to live in history! Do you understand me, brother?"

Edwin leaned back against the door. "You are mad, Wilkes! I truly believe you are mad!"

I stormed down the steps, and without looking back, I walked away from Edwin. I wondered at the words I had thrown at him about living in history. At the time, I did not even understand them myself, but now I do. I love my brother, and I would like to be able to include him in my plan, but I cannot. Alas, he would try to stop me, would even turn me, his own brother, over to the authorities. And he dares to call me mad!

Therein lies the end of the tale of the Booth brothers. No, wait, there is one more thing, and it's a stranger story than could ever be invented by a playwright for the stage. My brother Edwin saved the despicable Lincoln from losing his oldest son. It happened this way. Edwin, like Robert Lincoln, endeavored to buy a ticket at a crowded train station, New York or New Jersey, I believe. People pressed forward, and Lincoln's son was pushed up against a train that began to move. Robert Lincoln fell between the platform and the car, in danger of being crushed by the wheels of the moving train.

Quick as lightning, Edwin reached down and pulled the young man free. Robert Lincoln recognized Edwin and said something like, "Thank you, Mr. Booth." Soon the story was all over Washington City, young Lincoln being saved by the famous Edwin Booth. After my plan is carried out, whenever the rescue story is told, they will leave off Edwin's name, saying merely, "saved by the brother of John Wilkes Booth."

Oh, I've little doubt I would have done the same. The son cannot be blamed because his father is a tyrant. Yet it bothered me, knowing how glad Edwin was to have done something for Lincoln.

"Forget Edwin," I said aloud. "Think only of the

plan." Edwin could not call me mad if he knew how easily the whole thing had come to me.

When the carriage stopped in front of my hotel, I climbed down and began to pay Zeke. It was then that I started to shake. "You're dreadful cold, Mr. Booth," said Zeke. I did not tell him that it was excitement rather than the February cold that made me shake.

Far too keyed up to go to my room, I began to walk the streets of Washington City, dressed in my evening clothes. I laughed when people looked at me, wondering why I was dressed so. I found myself at the White House. I stood staring up at the second-floor balcony, and suddenly he was there. My heart beat loudly, so loudly that I thought if anyone were near me, he would surely hear.

It was a sign from God! Surely seeing the man standing there just at the moment when I looked up was a sign that my plan was as brilliant as I believed it to be. I put my hand over my heart to still it, and I gazed up at the devil of a man, shocked that there were no horns upon his head. Would the fools who support him change their minds if his evil were visible in such a way? Would my brother Edwin, for instance, say, "You know, Wilkes, there may be something to what you say about the fellow. I've noticed he has horns." But alas, there were no horns.

Not everyone can see him as he really is, but I do. I am the chosen one of God! I will take him, kidnap the man, ride with him to the South, and demand the release of those men who sit, cold and desolate, in prisons in the

North. One president for 35,000 men, an excellent idea! The idea of a genius!

The president did not even notice me, only looked over me just as he looks over all of humanity, unfeeling. "You will notice me, Mr. Lincoln!" I said under my breath. "You will notice me."

I walked on, oblivious to the cold, thinking, thinking! Money . . . money was needed. I was shorter of funds than usual. No matter, I had stock! Being part owner of oil fields in Pennsylvania would save the day for me and for the South.

I went back to my hotel, quickly changed my clothing, and headed for the brokerage house to sell my stock. "I need funds," I explained to the broker, "an investment much closer to my heart."

He nodded his understanding. "The theater, then, is it, financing a play, are you?"

"I am," I told him, and I did not lie. Did not Shakespeare say, "All the world's a stage, and all men and women merely players."

Yes, yes! That is exactly what Shakespeare said. My father lived his entire life playing roles created by Shakespeare. I have followed after him. At seventeen, I had the role of Richmond, young and heroic. I can remember that first echo of the trumpet, feel again the reverberation of the drum roll. Richmond is victorious. Richmond stops Richard III, evil king who would ruin his people. Ah, it is true, the people must be ever watchful, ever poised to strike down evil leaders. Even as a boy of seventeen I was of one mind with Shakespeare.

Suddenly, there in the brokerage house, I had another flash of insight! Richmond! Is it not significant that I played that role first? I was destined by God to be Richmond, not just on the stage, but in life. And the name. Oh, there *is* much in a name. The first part I played had the same name as does the capital of my beloved South.

I began my career in Baltimore, but it was only when I went to Richmond that I came into my own as an actor. It was the South that first loved me on the stage, and it is the South that I live for. It is the South that I will die for should it become necessary.

I left the brokerage house with funds, and as I left, I began remembering my classmates from military boarding school. We all wore gray uniforms, just as Southern troops do now. Some of the boys used to chide me. They were almost all from old Southern families, and they would sometimes tease me by saying Maryland was not truly part of the South, saying I was not one of them because my father did not own slaves.

"Some people in our state do own slaves," I told them. "My father sometimes rents them from other farmers to do work on our farm." I did not tell them that my father insisted that all servants in our house be treated as equals. I did not tell them that those rented slaves ate with us at the same table. I would have been too ashamed.

They will know soon, though, that I am a true son of

the South. My sweet mother was first to know that I would be important to my country. "I saw a vision," she told me when I was young. "It was shortly after your birth, and I had prayed to know your future. When I looked into the fire, there it was before me! As plain as the hand before my face, the flames flickered and danced to spell a word. The word was COUNTRY, Johnny, and I knew then that you were meant to be important to your country."

My mother never forgot her vision, and she has always wanted me to go into politics. Dear soul, she does not know that my true country is the Confederacy. She will! Yes, Mother, I am going into politics, going with everything I have.

My mother still calls me Johnny, as she did when I was a child, but my siblings have changed over to the name I prefer, Wilkes. I was named for John Wilkes, an Englishman who thought the crown was too powerful and wanted the people to have more rights, and I too am against enemies of the people.

"I won't be available for a time," I told my director when the stocks had been sold. "You will need to fill my role with the understudy." I turned to walk away, but his voice called after me.

"Wait." He rose from his chair and walked around his desk. "The understudy is no good."

"Well, perhaps he will improve with the chance to perform," I said, and I looked at my watch. "I have a train to catch," I explained, trying not to be impatient. "I am in need of a little rest. If the understudy is truly no good, get another actor."

"Another actor?" he repeated, and he began to pace, his hands on his temples. "There are no more actors!"

I was struck by the repeat of the phrase used after my father's death, but I did not take time to comment on the familiar words. "Nonsense," I said. "I see them daily, lined up and hopeful of an audition."

"There are no more J. Wilkes Booths to be found! I need you, man, can you not see that?"

"I am sorry, Lance," I said, "but this actor is in need of rest and a change of scenery. I am going to Canada." I walked away, then turned to him again. "But now that you have mentioned how vital I am, perhaps we should talk about more money when I return." I laughed.

The change of scenery outside my train window went unnoticed. I sat in my car, listening to the turn of the wheels on the track below. My eyes were closed, but I only pretended to sleep so as not to be disturbed. My mind raced. I would deposit the money in a Canadian bank, so that I could access the funds from anywhere. I would never be able to get at money in a Washington bank from the South. After the kidnapping, I would not be working for a time, only enjoying life in my beloved South.

Helpers! I must have help. There were men everywhere who supported the South, but I had to be careful, really careful. The men I selected must be completely trustworthy! Who could I trust without doubt?

Sam! I had not seen my old friend, Samuel Arnold, in thirteen years, but still I knew he would never betray me. We had been boys together at St. Timothy's School. Sam had fought for the South, and when his term of enlistment was up, he had returned to Baltimore. I would contact him at once.

Next, I thought of Michael, dear Michael O'Laughlin. We had been neighbors in Baltimore, had played many a summer day away together, and had studied together too. Michael was also in Baltimore. I would travel there to see them before I went back to the theater. Sam and Michael. I had known them always. They would, I believed, die before they would betray me. Enlisting my two old friends would be my first step. That decision made, I truly did let sleep come softly to my brain.

At first I dreamed of Southern soldiers, thousands of them in gray, rising up and marching, marching free, leaving their cold Northern prison walls behind. It was a sweet dream, but then it changed.

I was fifteen, back at school. Sam and I had gone to a country fair for a lark. The dream was a re-creation of an actual event. Everything was the same as it really was. We walked about drinking cider and trying our luck at a game of pitch and toss.

It was a spring night, and the air was full of the smell

of growing grass and of lilacs. At the edge of the fair stood a gypsy's wagon with a sign that advertised the telling of fortunes.

"Go have your future told, Wilkes," Sam said. "I know you think you will have fame."

I did go into the wagon. The woman was not old, but rather seemed not more than five or so years older than myself. She was pretty too. I could tell that even in the dim candlelight. Feeling generous, I paid her more coins than she asked for, laying them out on the table in front of her.

"Give me your hand," she said, and I did. Her expression grew troubled. "Oh," she said, "the lines, the lines!"

"What is it?" I demanded. "What is wrong with the lines?"

"I'd rather not say, sir," she murmured without looking up. She let go of my hand. "Take back your coins."

"I won't," I said, and I held out my palm to her. "Tell me."

"The lines are all crossed." She sighed deeply. "You will have a tragic life. You will be rich and generous with your money. You will be much loved." She shook her head slowly. "But you will die young, a terrible end."

A sort of cold feeling went over my entire body, but I gave myself a little shake and laughed. "Is my fate written in the stars, then?" I asked. "Is there nothing I can do to avoid this awful end?"

"I wish I had not seen your future," she told me. "Perchance if you turn missionary or priest." She shrugged her shoulders. "I cannot say for certain if that would change your fate."

I laughed again. "Well," said I, "I've overpaid you to tell me bad news."

"Take back your money, sir," she said, but I refused.

I was about to leave the wagon when she spoke again. "You have a handsome face, sir. It is tempted I am to follow after you because of your handsome face, but I won't, knowing your fate."

Outside Sam waited for me. "She said I would be rich and famous. She said I would be much loved." I made myself smile. "In fact she said I was so handsome she felt tempted to follow after me."

Sam slapped me on the shoulder. "I want to hear what she has to say about me," he said. I feared she might mention my ill fortune to him, but before I could think of anything to say by way of dissuading him, he had climbed the stairs to the open wagon door.

The woman came to the doorway. "I am closed," she said. "No more fortunes tonight."

"I'll pay well," said Sam, and he pulled coins from his pocket.

She shook her head and pointed down toward me. "I have told your friend's fortune," she said. "My powers are spent." She disappeared into the wagon and closed the door.

The dream ended there. I sat up straight and rubbed at

my eyes. It had been so like the real event, as if I had done the whole thing again. I had not thought of the evening in years, but now it all came back to me. I remembered how I had told no one what the gypsy said, but back in our room that night I waited until the other boys were asleep. I got up, took a paper and pen to the window. The moon was bright outside the glass. With the paper resting on the sill, I wrote out the gypsy's exact words.

I stayed at the window, going over the visit in my mind. The woman believed what she spoke, I was certain of that. Why else would she have reacted as she did and refused to tell Sam's fortune? I folded the paper. I would share the words only with my sister. That I did as soon as we were home together on summer vacation.

"You're actually worried by such nonsense? I can see that you are. Don't be foolish, Wilkes." Asia reached across the table to brush her fingertips against my cheek. "You, little brother, will have the best life of us all. The part about your being rich, famous, and loved I believe. Not because a gypsy said so, but because you are dear and special, the favorite of our parents, of us all." She took the paper from my hand and tore it into shreds. "There," she said, "now forget those foolish words. Let us have some fun."

I did forget them then, but sitting on the train, I remembered. Why had that dream come? I gave myself a small shake. It was because of Sam; thinking of Sam made me remember the fair, I told myself.

In Canada, the banker was glad to take my money even though he did not recognize my name or face. "I want my funds to be safe," I told him. "You never know when Southern soldiers will take our capital city."

He looked at me over the glasses that had slipped down his nose. "We are glad to have your business, sir," he said, "but surely there is no danger of Southern victory."

I rolled my eyes up toward heaven. "Oh, I pray you are right, but I am not so certain, not nearly so certain." I deposited my money and walked from the bank, a lover of the Union. Ah, yes, I am by profession an actor.

From Canada, I went straight to Baltimore, where I had arranged a meeting with my two old friends, both former soldiers for the Confederacy. We met in a Baltimore hotel room.

Sam arrived first. "Billy," he shouted when I opened the door, "Billy Bowlegs." I put out my hand, and he embraced me warmly. I knew when I heard him use that old nickname that our friendship was still the same. I knew I could persuade Sam to join me.

After Michael arrived, we had wine and cigars and much talk of the old days. I waited until just the right time to bring up my plans. I stood before them, my wineglass in my hand. "A magnificent design has come to me, friends," I said. "A magnificent way to change history. Would you like to be in on the plot, a plot more thrilling than any reenacted on the stage?" From the beginning they were with me, ready to pledge themselves at once.

Yes, I always had the power to lead them, and that power still existed.

Returning to Washington City, I went back to the stage, but my mind and heart were not with the lines I said. Telling everyone that I wanted to buy land, I rented a horse and rode out from Washington City. Out to the Maryland countryside I rode. "Maryland," I said aloud with only my horse to hear, "dear old Maryland of my birth. How sweet it would be to travel your roads for pleasure only, not for the dark business that sends me forth."

I found back roads and stopped to talk of purchasing property, an excuse to ride across the land of others, looking always for secret paths and spots hidden away from Union eyes. Maryland loves me, and I felt that love as I traveled her muddy roads.

I met one interesting person, Dr. Samuel A. Mudd, a young doctor who owns a huge estate with an acreage for sale. I asked to see the land, and I was put up for the night in the good doctor's home.

At dinner that night I said to the doctor, "I make no secret of my allegiance to the Confederacy."

"Why do you not fight for her, then?" questioned the man.

"I promised my mother," I told him. "I gave her my word that I would not be a soldier." I laughed. "But I did not promise that I would not be a spy, and I did not inform her that there are far bigger ways to serve the South than to wear a uniform, ways to change history."

"Lower your voice, man," said the doctor. "The servants may be listening. Such talk can be dangerous in Maryland."

I shrugged and said nothing more. I could see the doctor's face well in the light of the lamp. He had a fine Southern face and the eyes of a true gentleman.

I met the good doctor later in Washington City, and he asked if I knew John Surratt, a young man of twenty or so, and his mother. I told him that I had met the mother when a friend of mine lived in her boardinghouse. "I believe you and young Surratt have much in common," the doctor said, and he gave me a knowing smile and added, "Surratt has been a spy for the South."

He went with me to the boardinghouse, a place at 604 H Street. It was a tall building, with three floors and an attic. So many windows, like eyes looking out at me. I said as much to Dr. Mudd, who replied, "They are friendly eyes, Mr. Booth, eyes that look toward the South."

Mudd took me upstairs, where he introduced me to John Surratt. I liked him at once, and I began to speak to him of the plan. "Not now." The doctor put up his hand to stop me. "Don't talk in front of me. I want to know nothing." He left the room.

When the doctor was gone, I made a show of looking under the bed and in the wardrobe, opening the door to look out into the hall. "Do you want to hear my idea?" I asked Surratt, and I studied his intelligent face.

"I do," he replied.

I patted the pocket of my jacket. "I carry a gun, John," I said, "and I would not hesitate to use it on anyone who betrayed me."

He did not blink. "I would not betray you, sir, not as long as you act for the Confederacy."

I believed him, and I told him my plan to capture Lincoln. "Often he rides off to his Soldiers' Home cottage, using whatever army horse is available. He is seen alone on the streets frequently."

Surratt said he wanted time to consider the idea, but I knew as I went down the long front steps that he was with me. He had been with me from the beginning, only telling himself that a wise man always thinks over a proposition.

Surratt lived at the boardinghouse with his mother and sister Anna. The young woman hung about as I went to the front door to leave. She wished of course to speak to me, and so I smiled and said, "Hello." The girl was not unattractive, but I had no inclination to get involved, not with the serious business on my mind.

Besides, I looked down at the ring and remembered Lucy. Oh how I adore that name, but could I actually give up all other women? Well, how could I say what a year might bring to my life? Could I have both a place in history and the woman I love? I did not know, but I did know there was no time to think of women now.

Of course it was Lucy who got me a ticket to hear Lincoln's second inaugural speech. We could not go together because of her father. I stood on a stairway just behind and above the man as he spoke. "With malice towards none; with charity for all," he said, and I felt both my hands tighten into fists. I will show you malice, I thought, malice such as you have never known, sir.

It was after that second inaugural speech that the idea of using young Arabella Getchel came to me. At first I had not thought of using the girl, even though it was at the end of the ride with her that the idea came to me. Of course, using her made wonderful sense. She worked in the White House, had opportunity to come and go from there at will. No one would suspect anything if she returned there at night. Could she not hide somewhere near Lincoln, overhear his plans, or even ask him outright? She spoke to the man directly, did she not?

I was just entering Ford's Theatre when the idea came to me. Instead of going straight into rehearsal as I had planned, I turned down the back hall toward the costume shop. "Lillie, my love," I said to the costume mistress, "do you expect young Miss Arabella to come in today?"

Miss Lillie, a plump woman whose eyes were used to watching for missed stitches and misdeeds among actors, looked up at me from her sewing. "And why would you be asking?" she said. "If it's costume work you're in need of, tell me."

I had to think quickly, having no desire to arouse Lillie's suspicions of me. "I wanted to talk to her about her father," I said. "I've met a man who served for a time in

Delaware prison, and he said he knew a man named Getchel."

"Is that so?" she said, and she looked at me for a bit before going on. "Bella will be in for a time around five," she said, "that is, if she is not needed at the White House."

I smiled. "Of course, we must be second to the White House," I said, and I met Lillie's eyes directly until she looked away. My feelings about the Confederacy, I venture, were much discussed in Ford's Theatre, although, of course, no one said anything to me directly. Oh, it was no secret I favored the South, but they did not challenge me. I was, after all, the star.

Rehearsal was over around four thirty, but I stayed in the theater, busying myself by rearranging costumes in my trunks. I waited until a quarter past five to go to the costume shop. Arabella jumped from her chair when I entered the room. "Miss Lillie says you have news of my father," she cried.

Her eagerness both touched and encouraged me. "It is certainly because of your father that I wish to speak to you," I said, and turning to Lillie, I added, "if you can be excused from your work for a moment."

"Take her," said Lillie, "but I am warning you, Wilkes Booth, you trifle with that child, and you will have to answer to me. J. Wilkes Booth or not, I won't have it! Do you hear me?"

"Lillie, Lillie." I spoke gently. "Have you ever heard

tell of me taking advantage of any woman who did not know exactly what she was getting into?"

"Well, no, I suppose not, but Bella is only a child."

"She is," I said, smiling at the girl, "a beautiful child, but a child still. I would never harm a child." With that, I walked to Arabella, took her arm, and led her into the empty theater. "Let us sit in the middle row," I said to her. "What I want to discuss with you must not be overheard."

# 11

# ARABELLA

HER STORY

We all hoped that the war would be over before 1864 came to an end, but it was not. Each day Mr. Lincoln looked older, as if he too led the hard life his soldiers endured. The lines in his already craggy face seemed to deepen each day, and the sadness in his eyes was too much sometimes for me to see. I would turn my head from him and blink back tears. I wrote to Steven about him. "I worry that his heart may just explode with sorrow, his own and his country's. I wonder how long a man can live with such agony."

No one was barred from his door, and the line of people each day was long. Once on my way upstairs to the sewing room, I noticed a little girl waiting to see the president. I worked for several hours and came back down the stairs just as it was her turn to speak to Mr. Lincoln. "We don't usually have children here," said the secretary who sat at the door. "Why would a child need to see Mr. Lincoln?" The door was open, and from inside the room Mr. Lincoln called, "No, let the little maid speak to me."

I was very interested in what the girl could have to say to the president. She did not hesitate. "Mr. Lincoln," she said, "they are going to shoot my brother for falling asleep at his post. My mama and papa are gone now to the army post to say good-bye to him, but I came here. Please don't let my brother be killed. He is the only brother I have, sir, and my mama and papa will never stop crying if he dies."

Tears were rolling down the little girl's face, and she dropped to her knees, her hands folded beneath her chin as in prayer. I saw tears in the president's eyes too. He stood, went to the child, and put out his hand. "Get up, child," he said. "Your brother will live." She took his hand and kissed it.

He sat back down then and wrote a note and handed it to a waiting soldier. "Go with this man," he said to the child. "He will make sure your brother is pardoned. God knows I wish I could spare every mother and father the heartbreak of losing their boys."

The thought crossed my mind that I could go to Mr. Lincoln and ask him to pardon my father, but then I realized the president would want Father to promise not to go back into battle against Union soldiers. I knew my father would never make such a promise. I remembered the letter he had written to me.

"Dear Daughter," he wrote. "I am being allowed to write to you because you live in the North. I never thought I would be glad for that fact. I am ashamed that I did not come to retrieve you from your grandmother's house long ago. I was weak and let myself turn to drink to ease the pain of losing your mother. By the time I had pulled myself together, I felt too guilty to face you. I am a stronger man now, and I will come to take you home to Richmond if ever I am released from this prison. Life here is hard. We are often cold and unbelievably hungry. Some of the men have actually eaten rats. I have not yet found myself so desperate. Some men curse the day they ever enlisted in the army. I do not, and would gladly fight again for my beloved South."

Standing in the White House, I wondered how I would answer my father's letter. A week had passed since my receiving it, and I fretted, knowing he would be anxious for an answer. But what could I say? I no longer thought of Richmond as home. I also wondered how I would react to seeing my father, who I had longed for so desperately. Could I forgive him for neglecting me so? Yet I hurt at the idea that he was hungry and cold.

It was that very evening at Ford's Theatre that I first heard Wilkes's terrible proposal. I had just settled in for an hour of work when I saw him. He suggested that I go with

him into the theater. My heart raced because I thought he
had more news of my father.

There were no lights in the theater. Wilkes left the big
doors open so that light could come in. Still, it was dim.
Theater people, I had learned, called the rows of seats the
house, and it was there that Wilkes led me, to the middle
of the empty house.

"No one must hear our conversation," he said. He
stopped in the middle of a row, in the middle of the theater. "Sit down, Arabella," he said, "and tell me at once if
you see anyone." He sat backward in the seat beside me,
his body turned so that he could watch the other way.

He was quiet for a time after he was settled, and when
I could stand the silence no longer, I asked, "What is it?
What do you know about my father?"

He turned to look at me, reached out his hand, and
rested it against my cheek. "Tell me, sweet girl, are you my
friend?"

"Oh, yes . . ." I paused, then added, "Wilkes, I admire
you so much and feel fortunate beyond belief that you
would deem me worthy of a private conversation." I took
a deep breath and tried to relax and lean back in my seat.

He pressed his lips together hard. When he spoke, his
voice was low and thrilling. "Oh, yes, my dear, this is a
private conversation. It must ever be private, and you
must pledge to me that you will never tell anyone what we
discuss."

My head began to swim. Wilkes Booth was about to

take me into his confidence. The man who had been called "the most handsome man in America," sat beside me and asked me to share his secrets. I put my hand in the air to signify a pledge. "I will never tell a soul," I said. "I give you my most sacred pledge."

"Arabella," he said slowly, and the sound of his saying my name made me weak all over, "I need your help with a plan that is, undoubtedly, the most important thing to ever come into either of our lives. I need your help to save the South."

I felt a great coldness start in my feet and spread up into every part of my body. "To save the South?" I said weakly.

"Yes," he said. "I have a plan that may well give the South the upper hand in this war. You do want to save the South, don't you?"

What could I say to him? I could not bear to tell him the truth, that my sympathies now lay with the Union. He leaned toward me, and I could not stand to see him move away. "My father fought for the South," I said, stalling for time to think.

"I know," he said. "He suffers now in prison, but I have a plan that will ensure his release, and I need your help!"

"What could I do? I know nothing about the war, not really."

"Ah," said Wilkes, "but you do know about Mr. Lincoln."

I was dumbfounded. "The president?" I asked.

"Yes," he said, "the president, the man who caused this all, the man who now has tried to free the slaves." He threw his hands into the air. "What does he know of darkies? Can he not see that the colored man is better off as a slave? Has he not heard them singing in the fields as they work? Does he not understand that slavery has lifted them up from the conditions under which they lived in Africa? The man is a tyrant. He must be stopped."

I knew he was wrong. I had seen how Mr. Lincoln bore the burden of the war. He did not seem a tyrant to me. Remembering Mrs. Keckley, I knew he was wrong about slavery too. I remembered the scars on her back and how she had been used by her master. I said nothing. I could not have argued against him, no matter what he said. I pushed down any thoughts of my own, and listened only to the beauty of his voice, full and melodious.

He stopped talking and looked at me. "Where is your father being held?" he asked.

"Fort Delaware," I said.

"Ah," he said. "On Pea Patch Island, in the river that separates Delaware from New Jersey."

"You seem to know a lot about Fort Delaware," I said.

A sad look came to his face. "I know this, that a man who enters a military prison will be lucky if he gets out alive."

I gasped and moved to the edge of my chair. "He might be executed?"

Wilkes shrugged. "Well, I doubt that the guards are any too kind, but, no, it isn't likely they would hang him. The biggest danger is disease, smallpox and the like. Crammed in there as they are and weak from hunger, disease spreads like fire in a dry field of grass." He shook his head. "No, there's not much chance your father will live to see the war over."

"Oh," I said softly.

"But there is a way if you want to help him."

"Of course I do."

Wilkes leaned back then to rest against the seat in front of him. "There is a group of us, me and a few very close friends, who have determined to kidnap Mr. Lincoln. We would take him to Richmond, where he would be held and ultimately exchanged for all the Southern men in Northern prisons. With thirty-five thousand men to go back into the fields, the war would be over soon."

My head felt strange, as if I were dreaming the conversation. "What would happen to the president?"

"Lincoln? Oh, he would be treated well enough. I am sure the North would want proof that he was alive and well before making the deal. We have no plan to harm the man, though he mightily deserves it."

"What would happen if the South won the war?"

"America would be two nations. How could that hurt anyone?"

"But I don't understand what you would want me to do. How could I possibly help you?"

"You go daily to the White House. You must know that Mr. Lincoln frequently rides out to the Soldiers' Home, the hospital with his summer residence on the grounds. It is only a few miles from the White House, and he usually goes alone."

He reached out to take my arm, drawing me closer. He looked behind him again and then went on. "The place sits in a wooded area, a perfect spot for us to overtake him. If you got word to us when he plans to leave, we could go there, watch for his departure, and stop him. We could tie him in the back of the carriage, drive to the ferry over the Anacostia River. Fresh horses could be waiting for us, and we would ride on to cross the Potomac into Virginia."

A great relief went through my body. "He goes out there mostly after sundown. I am always gone home by then, or to Ford's to sew. I wouldn't be around to tell you."

Wilkes looked long and close at me, and then he smiled again. His smile was always something to behold, but this smile was even more special. Such a smile I had never seen; it seemed to flow over me like warm water, and I felt myself give in to it as I would to a relaxing bath. "It is simple," he said. "You must change your hours. Give up this place altogether." He put his hand into his pocket and brought out tickets. "I can easily supply you with theater tickets, more than you need." He pressed the tickets into my hand. "You tell the dressmaker you need to change your hours, that you are needed at home during the earlier hours and that she can leave work for you."

"Oh, Mrs. Keckley is mostly at the White House all day. Often she spends the night there. She does a great deal more for Mrs. Lincoln than just make clothes."

"Good, then, it should be perfectly fine with her if you come in to work later."

I was not so sure of the ease of it all. "I would have to drop my work at once if I saw Mr. Lincoln leave. How would I explain that to Mrs. Keckley?"

Wilkes laughed. "My dear girl," he said. "Have you not told me of your desire to act?"

"Yes," I said softly.

"Here then is a perfect opportunity to ply your art. Think of something! Become an actress!" The sound of footsteps behind him made him turn to look. "Oh," he said loudly enough to be heard, "here comes Wyatt, a producer. I've told him I want him to see you do your piece."

So it was that I found myself on the stage of Ford's Theatre, ready to recite "Annabel Lee" for Mr. Wyatt who took a seat about halfway back.

Wilkes stood leaning against the stage and looking up at me. "Speak up, now," he said softly, "and say it for me the way you did the other morning."

Somehow, I got Wilkes's suggestion about Mr. Lincoln out of my mind and put everything I had into the poem. I felt the thrill of the words. When I came to the last four lines, I thought my voice rose with just the right touch of passion.

> *"And so, all the night-tide, I lie down by the side*
> *Of my darling—my darling—my life and my bride,*
> *In the sepulcher there by the sea,*
> *In her tomb by the sounding sea."*

I curtsied slightly, and I heard, "Fine," come from where Mr. Wyatt sat. "Fine," he said again, and he clapped his hands. Next he rose and walked down to the stage, where he could look up to speak to me. "You're a lovely girl, and you have a good voice. Still, you've a lot to learn, of course," he said, "but the best way to learn is to watch real masters, like Booth here, at work. I'll find a small part for you soon." He took a piece of paper from his pocket. "Tell me your name again."

"Arabella," I said. "Arabella Getchel."

"Good," he said, and he spelled out my name, A-r-a-b-e-l-l-a G-e-t-c-h-e-l-l."

"One *l*, sir," I corrected him.

"Oh, right, must have it right when it goes up out front, aye?"

He was teasing me, I knew. It would be a long time before I could expect to see my name on a show card. Still, this was a beginning. A thrill passed through me. "Yes, sir," I said.

He turned back slightly to speak to Wilkes who had

come toward us. "And I suppose Booth here will know where to find you when that part for you comes along."

"Yes," said Wilkes. "I will know where to contact Arabella." He smiled up at me. "We are good friends."

After the producer took his leave, Wilkes looked at his watch. "I am late," he said. "I'm late for an engagement. Arabella," he said, "I will count on you to change your work schedule soon, but we must talk more." He paused and pursed his lips, thinking. "I have it," he said. "How would you like to have dinner with me tomorrow evening?"

"Dinner?" I asked as if I had never heard of the word.

"Yes," he said with a smile. "Dinner. You do eat the meal, do you not?"

Dinner with Wilkes Booth! Unable to speak, I merely nodded.

"Very well, then. Shall we say seven? Where shall I call for you?"

Suddenly the reality of what was being arranged came crashing in on me. "Oh, no," I said. "My grandmother would never hear of my going out in the evening with a theater man. Besides, I am afraid I have nothing suitable to wear." I looked down to touch my gingham dress. "This would certainly not do."

"You look lovely, my dear," Wilkes said warmly, and I felt my legs go weak. "You would be beautiful, I am sure, no matter what your attire." He smiled that special smile again. "But if you would feel better, take a dress from the costume shop. Don't worry about its owner. You can bring it back, and there are no shows here tomorrow." He took a notebook from his pocket, wrote a brief note, tore out the page, and gave it to me. "If Lillie or anyone else questions you, show them this, and as for your grandmother, perhaps you should meet me at my hotel, the National."

He was gone then with a wave and a quick good-bye. I stood on the stage, staring after him. My legs felt like jelly, and I wondered if I could actually climb down from the stage without falling. I was going to dinner with John Wilkes Booth!

With dreamlike motions, I made my way back to the costume shop. Relieved that Miss Lillie was not there, I went to a rack where three dresses hung. One, a beautiful red gown, looked about my size. Quickly I slipped it into a box, and with the box under my arm I hurried from the theater.

At home I told Grandmother that I had brought a dress from Ford's to take with me to Mrs. Keckley to ask her advice about an alteration. Relieved that Grandmother did not ask more questions, I slid the box out of sight under my bed.

"You're quiet, child," Grandmother said while we ate our evening meal. "Is something troubling you?" She peered closely at me as she dipped beans onto my plate.

Unable to meet her gaze, I looked down at my food. "Just tired," I said. The truth, though, was that I had never been less tired. In bed that night, I lay wide-eyed, a thousand thoughts going through my head. What would I tell Wilkes when he demanded an answer about my helping him kidnap Mr. Lincoln? I couldn't do such a thing, could I? But how could I say no? Wilkes wanted to take me to dinner! He could have arranged to talk to me again at the theater, but he wanted to take me to dinner! He must like me, must want to spend time with me! Besides there was my father to consider. Shouldn't I grab at a chance to help him?

I rolled about in my bed. I needed to sleep, needed to be fresh for tomorrow. I told myself not to think about Wilkes or his plan. Steven, I would think about Steven, but then I began to think of how Steven would hate Wilkes's plan, would hate my being involved. Steven would not like my going out in the evening to meet Wilkes either.

I decided not to think about Steven. He was dear, my closest friend, and I loved him with all my heart. Steven would always be there for me, wouldn't he? I knew Wilkes would not be a permanent part of my life, but why not enjoy the marvelous chance to know him? No other man was like Wilkes Booth. One look from Wilkes, and my body felt limp.

Finally, I let myself think of Wilkes without restraint. I imagined myself in the red gown, being held in his arms. I imagined our lips meeting in a kiss. Going over and over the scene in my mind, I finally fell asleep.

Despite the shortness of the night, I was up early at

dawn next day, and I went early to the White House. I was already at work when Mrs. Keckley came into the sewing room. I had practiced what I would say to her about the red gown. "I have a chance to go to a hotel dining room with some theater people," I said. "It is an opportunity to actually spend time with an actress and actor who might be able to get me an audition." I reached for the box that I had placed on the table beside me. "I've borrowed a dress, and I am hoping you will let me try it on, see if it needs altering."

Mrs. Keckley agreed, and I tried on the dress, which was too large in the waist. Mrs. Keckley pinned it for me, and I knew I could take the stitches out tomorrow. "Where are you going to dinner?" she asked as she worked.

I had been studying myself in the long mirror. The dress made me feel beautiful, and I could see that my face had a glow to it. I barely knew that Mrs. Keckley had spoken. "I'm sorry," I said. "What did you say?"

"I asked where you were eating tonight."

"At the National Hotel. Doesn't that sound grand?"

"Uh-huh." She put in the last pin. "There," she said and stepped back to look at me. "You look lovely, Bella," she said, but I noticed a worried look in her eyes. "You want to be careful with folks, honey, not just theater folks, but all kinds. You want to be sure who is your true friend, and who would drop you like a hot potato if trouble should come."

"Oh, I know," I said. "I know." But of course I did not

know, could not see what heartbreak lay ahead for me, could not see that I was being flattered into doing what I knew was wrong. "I am always careful about people," I told Mrs. Keckley. I thanked her then for helping me and got down from the fitting platform.

All day I watched the clock. At six I usually went home for the day or to Ford's to sew. This day, I would put on the red dress again and go off to meet a prince. Thinking I was at the theater, my grandmother would not wonder about my absence. She would leave a plate of food for me on the stove, but I would not be hungry when I arrived home. I felt magnificent, as if I might never need to eat or sleep again.

I dressed in the sewing room, put my hair on top of my head, and with my savings, I hired a hansom cab to take me to the National Hotel. I had, I believed, no need to worry about how I would get home. Wilkes would see that I arrived safely at my door when our magnificent evening was over. Even before I got to the room, I heard the music, wonderful sweet violin music.

He sat at a table facing the door, and when I entered he got up and came toward me, his hand out to take mine. I felt as if I floated toward him. He took my hand and kissed it. "Let's have our dinner first," he said when we were settled at our table. "There will be time enough to talk business when our meal is finished."

Wilkes ordered for me, duck cooked in wine sauce. The food was wonderful, but I had absolutely no hunger

and had to force myself to eat. As we ate, he told me stories, stories about the theater and about growing up with
his brothers and sisters. "Once," he said, "when we lived
on the farm, I took it into my head that I could be a good
actor if I could portray a woman." He laughed. "My
sister Asia, always ready to help me, worked with me on
how to walk. She told me I was good and suggested that I
should try to fool the slaves from the next place that we
always rented to help with the harvest. They knew me
well, and I worried that I might not pass the test. I put on
one of Asia's bonnets and went out into the fields. The
men paused in their work as I passed them. They took off
their hats and bowed their heads in respect." He laughed
again and slapped the table. "Not wanting to embarrass
them, I did not let on, only walked away with my head
held high. I knew from that time that I could act." He
sighed. "We had good times together, especially Asia and
I." He leaned toward me. "Do you have brothers and sisters, Bella?"

I shook my head. "No, I had a rather lonely childhood," I said, "after my mother died, that is."

He reached across the table and took my hand. "You
will be lonely no more, sweet thing. You now have Wilkes
Booth for a friend."

It seems strange to me now that at just that moment,
just when Wilkes was speaking of being my friend, and I
was thrilling to the idea, that I should look up and see my
real friend. I had not expected to see Steven until August,

but there he was, standing in the doorway to the dining room at the National Hotel.

"Oh!" I gasped and put my hand over my mouth. Steven moved his head in one direction and then the other, obviously looking for me. He was looking for the Bella he knew in a simple dress, her hair down. I knew he would eventually spot me, and I did not want him to come to our table. "I must speak to someone," I said. "I'll be right back." Jumping up hurriedly, I bumped against the table as I stood, but I did not take time to say "Excuse me" to Wilkes, who rose, as a gentleman would, until I had moved away.

Steven's face lit up with a smile when he saw me, and he started to move toward me. I held up my hand to motion for him to stop, and I went to him. He took my hand, "Wow, Bella," he said, "you are sure dressed up! You look beautiful. What are you doing?"

"Let's talk in the hall," I said, and I led Steven out of the dining room.

Steven, still the talker, did not wait for me to answer his question. "Boy," he said, "am I glad I found you! When you weren't home, I went to Ford's Theatre, but I couldn't get in there, so I checked the White House. Mrs. Keckley said I might find you here."

"Yes," I said, glancing over my shoulder toward the dining room entrance. "I'm with a gentleman—he's an important actor, and we're talking about a role that might come up for me soon." My voice sounded strange in my ears. I could not look at Steven's face. He knew me so well, and I realized at once that he would know I was lying.

He bit at his lip before he spoke. "Gosh, that's great, I guess, him wanting to get you a part and all." He leaned around me slightly as if to get another look into the dining room. "If you aren't finished eating, I could wait here in the lobby for you. Have you talked over the part enough?"

I wanted to stall, needed time to think of something to say. "How did you get here?" I asked. "I thought you were coming in the summer."

"I got a chance for a free trip, riding down on the train with one of the younger students who needed to come to Washington for a funeral. I've got to go back early in the morning, got to get back to class."

I could have asked Steven to wait for me in the lobby, could have excused myself after the meal. The evening would still have been young enough for me to spend some time with Steven. I thought of all that, but I also thought of being driven home in Wilkes's carriage. A scene flashed through my mind of Wilkes's kissing me good night.

"I can't just leave after the meal," I said to Steven. "It would be rude not to let the gentleman see me home."

A look of pain crossed Steven's face. "Bella," he said, "tell me there is nothing personal between you and this man. Why should he care who sees you home?"

"We could meet in the morning," I said. I reached out to pull at his arm. "I don't care how early."

The familiar blue eyes went cold, colder than I had ever seen them. "Never mind," he said, and he turned sharply to go.

Suddenly, I was desperately afraid of losing him. I could not let him go away angry with me, and I ran after him. "Steven," I pleaded, "just a minute." He did not turn back.

I held tight to the back of a couch in the lobby for a moment. I had hurt Steven's feelings. What if he would not forgive me? Hadn't I said to Wilkes in the cab that winter morning that I could not imagine my life without Steven? I knew him to be a stubborn person, once he made a decision. I gave myself a little shake. I would not think about life without Steven now. If I did, I might run out and leave the most handsome man in America waiting for me. I would have time later to sort it all out.

I put my hand to my hair and smoothed back some wisps that had fallen from the combs. I squared my shoulders and walked back into the dining room.

Wilkes rose as I came to the table. "I was near to worrying about you," he said.

I smiled. "It was nothing, a friend happened by. I hadn't seen him for a while and wanted to say hello. That's all."

"Good," said Wilkes, and he pulled his chair close to mine. "We need to talk some business now."

There was no one at the table near us, but still Wilkes's voice was low. "Now, as I said, you need to change your work hours. Be ever watchful of the president. When he rides out to the Soldiers' Home, all you have to do is leave at once. Go to the Surratt boardinghouse and ask for John Surratt. When he comes to the door, tell him you were sent by Wilkes Booth. Then you can go home. Your part will be over, and you will have done something fine for your father and for the South."

I wanted to say no. Wanted to say that I did not care to get involved in such a plot. "What if this John Surratt is not at home? What would I do then?"

Wilkes smiled. "Don't worry, he will be there, and he will know where to reach me."

"Wouldn't it be better to have the man watch the White House in the evenings? I might miss Mr. Lincoln's leaving."

Wilkes reached out to touch my face. "We can't have men seen watching the White House," he said. "They would be noticed. Don't worry your pretty head with details." He looked at me closely, then drew somewhat away from me. "You do want to help me, don't you? You do want to save your father?"

My cheek burned where his fingertips had brushed it. I could not bear to have him move away from me. "Yes," I said softly. "Yes, I will do what you say."

He put his arm around my shoulders and squeezed me close to him for just an instant. "We will work happily together, Arabella," he said. I drew in the smell of his skin and wanted nothing else except to stay there close to him.

He hailed a hansom cab for our ride home. He helped me up, and I took a seat on one side as he climbed in behind me. I wondered if he would sit on the seat across from me, but he settled himself beside me, just close enough so that we bumped into each other when the carriage went around a corner. I felt like Cinderella returning from the ball, but in my case the prince was with me, not left holding my shoe.

Wilkes told me theater stories. "I played with a company in Philadelphia when I first started," he said. "There I was onstage during the second performance when my fake mustache came loose as I kissed a woman on the cheek. Stuck right to her skin, but strangely she failed to notice. She moved away after the kiss. I was supposed to stay still, but I followed her, my hand over my mouth in a foolish attempt to hide my bare upper lip. I wanted to get close enough to her to brush the mustache from her face, but she was trying to talk to another character who had come onto the stage. She gave me angry looks for being where I was not supposed to be and moved away each time I got close. Finally, I lost control. "My mustache is stuck to your cheek," I said in what I intended to be a whisper. It came out loud, though, because I worked so hard in those days at projecting to be heard. The audience roared with laughter. I wished a trapdoor could open and swallow me up!"

"It must be wonderful to be onstage, to have stories about being in plays," I said.

He reached for my hand and squeezed it. "Ah, you will know, Arabella. You will be one of us and win many a heart."

His was the only heart I wanted to win. I knew I had lost touch with reality. Even there in that carriage, as we rode toward my home, I knew I was making a mistake, but I seemed to have no power to stop myself. When we arrived, Wilkes walked with me to the door. I did not want my wonderful evening to end. We stood on the stoop in the moonlight, and Wilkes pushed a fallen wisp of curl back from my forehead. His face was close to mine. "Tomorrow you must change your work schedule. Then when the time comes, run quickly to the Surratt boarding-house. Knock on the door and say simply, 'Wilkes sent me.' Nothing more will be required of you." He moved as if to step away, and then he turned back. "Tell me once more that I can count on you. That you are my friend and will not fail me."

For a second, I did not speak. "Arabella?" he said, and his voice was soft and sadly sweet.

"Yes," I said. "Oh, yes, I am your friend, and I will do exactly as you ask."

"Good," he said. He put his hands on both sides of my cheeks, tilted my head slightly up to meet his, and kissed me briefly on the forehead. "I knew I could count on you. I must run." He walked back toward the carriage then, leaving me still on the stoop. After a few steps, he turned back and threw me a kiss.

For the second night in a row, I slept but little. Grand-mother had not stirred as I slipped out of the red dress and folded it back into the box. I went immediately to my bed, but sleep did not come. I lay there going over the evening. Away from Wilkes, as I now was, my thoughts turned to Steven. In my mind I saw the hurt look on his face. As the night hours passed, my feelings for Wilkes seemed more and more like a dream, and my misery grew over what I had done to Steven and about what I had agreed to do to Mr. Lincoln.

What would happen, I wondered, if I did not do as I had promised Wilkes? He would find me, I knew, and demand to know why I had changed my mind. It did not seem likely I would have the strength to stand against him. There was my father to consider also, and Wilkes had promised that no harm would come to Mr. Lincoln.

I walked to the White House the next morning full of dread. What would I say to Mrs. Keckley? That part proved easy. I simply told her that I had given up sewing at Ford's for a time and had taken on a dressmaking job for a woman who lived near me. I would need to come to the White House later. I held my breath after the request was made.

She stood beside a dressmaker's dummy, making tucks in a blue gown. She looked up at me and smiled. "Certainly," she said. "I'll be glad to have your company while the Lincolns are at dinner."

I was unaccustomed to lying, and I looked down at

my feet as she spoke. "Is something more troubling you, Bella?" she asked.

"No," I said, but I was troubled, troubled beyond any trouble that had ever touched my life. On the second day, I was about to enter the White House when a boy came running toward me waving an envelope. "Arabella Getchel?" he called. "I've been waiting for you." He handed me the envelope.

"It's from Mr. Booth," he said with pride. "He paid me extra." The boy moved away then. I took a small piece of expensive-looking paper from the envelope. "I pray you have not forgotten our cause," it said, and it was signed, "Your admirer, W. B."

Smiling, I slipped the note into my pocket. Wilkes was my admirer. I had done the right thing to agree to his plan. I pushed down the pain I had been feeling over Steven. I would think only of Wilkes. I had an opportunity to be his friend, to spend time with him, an opportunity that hundreds of women would love to have.

Several days passed. I watched Mr. Lincoln as closely as possible. His personal office was just across the hall from our sewing room. Often our door was ajar, and I moved about, keeping my eyes open. Mrs. Lincoln sometimes came into the sewing room after her evening meal. She would take off her shoes, stretch herself on the fainting couch, and talk to Mrs. Keckley. I kept to my work, listening.

On the fourth evening, my waiting was over. Mrs. Lincoln came in, and with a sigh, she headed for her couch. "It's been a hard day for Mr. Lincoln," she said. "Lizzie, I sometimes think he will just fall dead of exhaustion. Thank God for the Soldiers' Home." My eyes were up, but Mrs. Lincoln put her head against the back of the couch and closed her eyes before she went on. "He's riding out this evening. Dear Heaven, I hope he is able to rest there."

I fought the urge to gasp. Mrs. Keckley put down her work and went to Mrs. Lincoln. "Does your head ache?" she asked.

"Oh, yes, Lizzie, would you massage my temples?"

I studied the button I had just attached. My plan had been to pretend sickness when I heard what I had waited for, but I changed my mind. I rose and went to Mrs. Keckley. "Mrs. Lincoln's headache makes me think of my grandmother. She was unwell when I left her, and I suddenly feel I should go home to check on her," I said softly.

Mrs. Keckley nodded. "No need to come back this evening," she whispered, and she continued to stroke Mrs. Lincoln's head.

I left the room quickly. In the hall I met the president. "Evening, Bella," he said to me.

Wishing for all the world that I had not had to see that weary face, I nodded a greeting and hurried down the stairs.

# 12

# WILKES

## HIS STORY

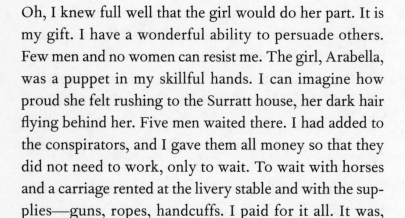

Oh, I knew full well that the girl would do her part. It is my gift. I have a wonderful ability to persuade others. Few men and no women can resist me. The girl, Arabella, was a puppet in my skillful hands. I can imagine how proud she felt rushing to the Surratt house, her dark hair flying behind her. Five men waited there. I had added to the conspirators, and I gave them all money so that they did not need to work, only to wait. To wait with horses and a carriage rented at the livery stable and with the supplies—guns, ropes, handcuffs. I paid for it all. It was, after all, *my* scheme, *my* grand plan to save my beloved South!

As soon as the notice came, four of them rode out toward the Soldiers' Home, taking the back roads, so as not to be noticed. The fourth man came for me at the National Hotel.

My heart raced as fast as the horses' hooves as we rode out of Washington City. I looked back only once over my shoulder and saw the outline of the Capitol Building rising above the other buildings like a mountain. I hoped to never see the city again. After the war finally ended, I would resume my acting, but only in the South. I would be a hero, more adored than Jefferson Davis or Robert E. Lee. Crowds would shout my name and wave flags when they saw me. If my brothers or even my dear mother ever wanted to see me again, they would need to travel into the Confederate States of America. Even Asia would have to come to me.

I felt a pain as I thought of Lucy. She knew of my love for the South, but how would she take it when she learned I had kidnapped Lincoln? Her father would never agree now that we should be wed. She was the strongest woman I had ever known. Perhaps she would have the courage to defy him? I hoped so, but as I looked back over my shoulder, I knew I might be saying good-bye to Lucy. Well, had I not pledged my life to this cause?

"Faster," I urged my horse on. He tried, but I did not feel one with him. I thought of my dear pony, Cola. If he had been with me, the race toward my destiny would have been even sweeter.

We met our band at the designated spot in the woods,

just out of sight of the Soldiers' Home. The plan was already being carried out. Arnold had moved closer to the house, where he would watch from behind a tree. When the president left the house, he would run to tell us. The horses were kept ready. We would ride around the back roads and surprise Mr. Lincoln's horse on the curve.

Hours passed. We spread our blankets on the ground. I could not sleep, but I heard snores coming from the other three. After four hours, I woke Michael and told him to take over Sam Arnold's watch. Dawn came with no movement from the house. Despair washed through me. "He is not in there," I said, and cursing, I kicked at the earth beneath my shoes. "Obviously the man never came here. Something must have changed his mind."

Heads down, we made our way back into the city, and there we learned what had caused the president to abandon his plans. "Richmond falls!" I heard a newspaper boy shout in front of my hotel. I jumped from my horse, unmindful of the reins. It had started away when Michael caught it, but I cared not what became of the rented horse. My only interest was the paperboy.

He was a small boy with a thin face. Grabbing his arm, I yelled, "What are you talking about? Why are you shouting about Richmond?"

The boy wrenched his arm free. "It's true, mister." He held up the paper and pointed to the headlines. "The rebs done been chased out of Richmond. I reckon the war is most near over."

"What makes you an authority on war?" I demanded. I jerked a paper from his hand and gave him a handful of coins, more than the cost of the paper.

"Thank you, mister," he called after me, but I was already going through the hotel door.

Michael followed me. "What are we going to do now, Billy?" he asked. "Are we going to try again?"

"Go get some sleep," I said without looking at him. "I will come to you later."

In my room, I did not have the strength to walk even to a chair or the bed, falling instead onto the floor. I spread the paper on the purple carpet before me, and read, tears streaming down my face. Richmond had indeed fallen to the Union troops. The brave people of Richmond, though, had not given in easily, burning much of their beautiful city so that the Union would capture mostly damaged property.

The new capital of the Confederacy was moved to Danville, Virginia. I stared at the paper. "Danville," I said aloud. "I have never even been to Danville." I did not go to the Surratt house, having no wish to face the others, having no wish to answer their "What now?"

I went instead to an establishment that I frequented. I did not speak to the proprietor or smile at the other customers as usual. I settled myself on a stool and ordered one drink after another, never looking up or around me. I drank until I began to forget. Then I stumbled out, went back to the hotel, and fell fully clothed onto my bed. When next I woke, it was late morning. I washed myself and was going out for a meal when I saw the same paperboy at the edge of the street. No doubt remembering my generosity of the day before, he came toward me.

"What's the news today?" I asked.

"Mr. Lincoln's gone to Richmond," he said, and he held out a paper to me, his eyes bright.

"That's not a subject I'd care to read about," said I, but I reached into my pocket to find coins for him anyway.

"He will be back," I told my friends later at the Surratt house. "He will have to come back, and we will be ready." I looked from one doubtful face to the other. "Don't be downhearted, boys," I said a good deal more cheerfully than I actually felt. "We are a long way from being beaten. We'll get the fiend yet!"

We didn't, though, not as we had planned. Details had to be worked out all over again, and my men were hesitant, especially Sam. "Why not wait, Billy?" he argued. "Let's see what happens for a few days."

I looked at them, one face after the other, I looked at them there in that room, sitting on the edge of a bed or on the floor, leaning against the wall, and I knew the terrible truth. They had been relieved when we had failed to capture him. They had lost heart. I would find a way to rouse their patriotic blood again, a way to give them courage.

I took money from my purse and passed it out among them. "Relax a bit, boys," I said. "But do your drinking only here among your brothers. Drinking might loosen your tongues." I stopped and looked at each face again. "He whose tongue gets loose will die," I said, and I put my hand inside my coat where they knew I kept my revolver. I did not speak harshly, only evenly and with conviction. They knew I did not make idle threats.

The next morning, April 10, I, like the rest of Washington City, woke to the ringing of bells. The sound shook me from sleep. I ran to the window to confirm what I thought was true; only a pink glow could be seen to the east. It was not yet dawn. "What in blazes has happened at the churches?" I asked aloud, and then suddenly I knew. A sound, the saddest, I think, that has ever come from me, rose in my throat and mixed with the wild ringing of the terrible bells.

Pulling on my pants but not bothering with a shirt or coat, I stumbled out onto the street. People poured from every door, women still in nightgowns, men half dressed. "The war is over, friend," a man near my hotel door said to me, and he reached as if to embrace me. I shoved him away. My legs seemed as dead as my heart felt, but I staggered into the street.

People danced and shouted. Grown men cried, tears of joy rolling down their pitiful faces as if they were babies. "Let us thank God," one man shouted, and a dozen or more people knelt there in the middle of the street.

Saloon owners threw open their doors, and men entered, making toasts as the dawn came, toasts to General Grant, toasts to Abraham Lincoln, toasts to the United

States of America. For once I did not want to drink. At first I wanted to die. I moved among the celebrating people, and I wanted to die. My revolver was back in my room. Perhaps, I thought, I should get it. Perhaps I should kill myself before the day fully came, the first full day of defeat. Only thoughts of my mother, Lucy, and Asia stopped me.

Numbly, I made my way back to my room. Falling on my bed, I began to cry. If only, I thought, if only I could be in the South now to mourn with my people. I cried far more than I had when my father died. This loss was bigger than my father, bigger than my own little life.

When I had no more tears to shed, I went to my bureau and rummaged until my fingers found the small envelope of sleeping powders I had been given by a doctor when troubled with insomnia a few months earlier. Thankfully, I downed them, and fell into a wonderful, dreamless sleep.

I did not go out of my room until April 11. I went to a good tavern and ate a large meal of beef and vegetables, my first food since the day before yesterday. Then I went to the Surratt house to see how my companions fared. No one was to be found except David Herold and Lewis Powell.

"Well, boys," I said to them, "I will confess to you that I was brought low by the news of Lee's surrender. I let myself fall into deep despair, but I am back now." I slapped the gloves I held in one hand against the palm of the other. "All may not be lost."

"Not lost?" said Herold, and he looked up at me with such admiration, I had to glance away. Herold was young, not yet twenty, and to him my twenty-six years were to be admired.

Powell admired me too, saw me as a wise and widely successful man. The adoration in their eyes cheered me. "Up with you, men," I said. "They say Mr. Lincoln is about to speak from a White House balcony. Let us go hear what the man has to say."

Candles burned in every window of a government building, bands played, crowds cheered. Lincoln stood reading a speech by the light of a candle held for him. He talked of letting the Southern states back into the Union if 10 percent of the voters would take a pledge of allegiance to it. "Allegiance to the Union," I whispered, and the words left a sour, sickening taste in my mouth.

Lincoln's son sat on the balcony floor at his father's feet, catching the sheets that were dropped as the president finished with them. "What is the child doing here?" I said to my companions. "The man does not even know how to give a speech in a serious manner!"

Lincoln began to talk about the possibility of giving some of the former slaves the vote. The thought enraged me. "That does it," I said. "He is picking up where old John Brown left off. Brown was a criminal. What does that make Lincoln?" I raised my fist in the air and shook it.

People were looking at me, and my companions tried to hush me. They began to lead me away. "Let this be the last speech the man ever makes," I shouted, too blinded by fury to care who heard me.

When we were well away from the crowd, Powell spoke. "You could have put us into a real mess, talking so where people could hear."

I only looked at him and said nothing. "What do you mean, it is the last speech he will ever give?" he asked.

"You two go back to the Surratt house," I snapped, "and wait for me. I don't pay you to tell me to be quiet. I pay you to be ready when I need you." I saw defiance in their faces, and immediately I knew I had gone too far. I need to use charm with these two, just as I used it onstage. I wiped my hand over my face. "Forgive me, friends," I uttered. "I have had too much to drink, and I have had too much sorrow, far too much sorrow. My brain is fuzzy. I need rest. When I have refreshed my spirit, we will talk more."

For two days, the twelfth and thirteenth of April, the images are blurred in my mind, blurred with whiskey and despair, but on the fourteenth day of April I awoke with a clear head. I had not received any mail for some time, so I dressed and walked to Ford's Theatre, where all my mail was sent while I stayed in Washington City.

As soon as I entered the big building, I knew something was going on. James and Harry Ford, brothers of the owner, scurried about giving orders to workmen who worked to separate boxes seven and eight, the best seats in the house. "Why all this?" I asked Harry.

"The president and Mrs. Lincoln are coming tonight," he told me over his shoulder, "and bringing guests, maybe General Grant and his wife."

I stepped back to lean against a wall. My entire body had gone weak with sudden knowledge and determination. Here was my chance, my duty. Here in Ford's Theatre, the building that had been a home to me, I would make my move. Here I would claim my destiny.

Still unable to walk far, I made my way to a chair just outside the box where I pretended to busy myself with my mail, but where I was able to watch as they carried comfortable chairs, a sofa, and a rocking chair with a red upholstered seat into the box. "Mr. Lincoln always sits in this one," I heard James Ford say to the man who carried the rocking chair.

When the furniture was arranged, they busied themselves with decorating the front of the box. They draped sheets of red, white, and blue cloth from one corner to the other. A flag stand was secured to the box, and a big flag put in it. The last preparation was a large portrait of George Washington that was fastened to the center of the box.

When the men were finished and gone about other tasks, I slipped quietly into the small hall that led to the box. I would need to drill a hole in the door of the box, so that I could look through and be sure of the right moment to enter.

I went down to the shop where scenery was made to

find a tool with which to drill. I was reaching for the drill when I heard the girl's voice.

"Wilkes," she said. "I came here hoping to see you."

I whirled around to see Arabella Getchel. My impulse was to brush her off quickly. She was not needed in this new venture, and her presence would be a liability. I steadied myself, though, before I spoke. Better to get rid of her gently. "Arabella," I said, and I smiled. "How good to see you."

"I've wanted to see you," she said, "since——" She frowned first, and then her face brightened. "Well, things didn't turn out as you planned," she said, "but at least now all the prisoners will go free just as you wanted."

The strain of the last few days overtook me, and something inside me snapped. "You foolish, simpering child," I thundered. "Did you think that is all I wanted? Just to free the prisoners? Didn't you know that my plan was to ensure victory for the Confederates?"

She stepped back from me. "You needn't be so hateful," she said. "You should be glad your plot did not work. Kidnapping a president is a dangerous thing."

Wild with anger, I pulled my revolver from my pocket. "Dangerous? What do I care for danger? There are much bigger issues at risk. I am about to change the course of history."

I realized at once that I had gone too far, but it was too late. The girl turned to run, but I was quicker than she. I lunged after her, grabbing her arm and twisting it behind her.

She cried out in pain. I put the gun to her temple. "Hush, Arabella," I said. "Screaming will only force me to shoot you. Besides, the workers are all gone. Only you and I are in this whole big building now. Just us two. If I let you go, you will run to the authorities, won't you? Never mind answering, I know full well that you would."

# 13

# ARABELLA

HER STORY

---

I ran all the way to the Surratt house to tell those men that Mr. Lincoln was going to the Soldiers' Home. I walked home slowly, though, and as I walked, the truth of what I had done settled over me. I had helped to kidnap the president, a fine, gentle man who had been nothing but kind to me. I had also turned my back on my best friend. I did not ask myself why I had done such terrible things. I knew the answer. I had fallen completely under the spell of an actor. Wilkes had said nothing about seeing me again. He wouldn't be able to come back to Washington City, ever. Because a handsome, famous man had been kind to me, I had seemingly lost all control.

I did not know that a message came just as the president was leaving. I did not know that the fall of Richmond made Mr. Lincoln's plans change.

Had I known, I would no doubt still have felt guilty over what had almost happened, but probably I would not have tossed and turned all night in misery, unable to sleep, unable to forgive myself for my actions. The next morning I could eat nothing for breakfast. "Are you sick, Bella?" Grandmother wanted to know.

I nodded my head. Then I folded my arms on the table, rested my head on my arms, and cried. "Child, child," said my grandmother. "What is it?"

"I'm worried about Father," I lied. Then I got up and ran from the house. I had not taken a coat, and the early April morning was cool. Without deciding to do so, I headed for the White House. I was about to cut around to the back when I saw Mr. Lincoln step out onto the balcony.

Suddenly I didn't feel cold anymore, and the smell of the lilacs growing nearby filled the air. The president stood on the balcony for a moment, put out his arms, and seemed to be drawing in a deep breath of air. I hoped he could smell the lilacs too. A great joy flooded through me, and I clapped my hands. With a singing heart, I ran to the back entrance and up to the second floor.

"Have you heard the news, Bella?" Mrs. Keckley asked as I entered the sewing room, and I listened as she told me all about Richmond. "The president is planning to go there," she said. Then she remembered why I had left early the day before. "How is your grandmother?" she asked.

"Much improved," I said. "Isn't this a wonderful spring day?"

"It is," she said, and she smiled at me. "It is also a day when we have work to do. The war may be over any day now. Mrs. Lincoln will need dresses to wear for celebrations."

Later, while Mrs. Lincoln tried on a white dress with red flowers so Mrs. Keckley could make adjustments, the president came into the room. It was not unusual for him to come into the sewing room when Mrs. Lincoln was there. It gave them a chance for a brief conversation in the middle of a busy day. No one looked for him there, and he could relax by partially stretching out on the fainting couch for a few minutes' rest.

He had been relaxing for a few minutes when he sat up and rubbed his eyes. "Mother," he said to Mrs. Lincoln, "did I tell you about the dream I had last night?"

"No," she said. "You did not. Was it a nice dream?"

He shook his head. "No, it was not a pleasant dream, not at all. I dreamed that I woke from a sleep, here in the White House. I knew at once that something was wrong and was not surprised when I began to hear sobs, subdued but definite. I put on a dressing gown and walked down the hall to see who was crying.

"The sobs grew louder, and I knew many people were crying. I made my way down the stairs to the East

Room. I opened the door slowly and saw that the room was full of mourners. At the center of the room stood a casket with soldiers standing all about it. A soldier also stood by the door.

"I went to him and asked quietly, 'Tell me, please, who is dead in the White House?'

"The young man turned to me, and with tears in his eyes, he said, 'Why, it's the president. Mr. Abraham Lincoln is dead, killed by an assassin.'

"Just then the sobs grew louder, and they awakened me. There I was in my bed, not dead at all, but I can tell you, Mother, the dream disturbed me. It really did."

At such times, when the Lincolns talked to one another, Mrs. Keckley and I kept our heads down, our eyes on our sewing as if we were not there, but this time I could not keep from glancing up at Mrs. Lincoln. She was a woman who always had color in her cheeks, but her face had grown white, her eyes big and frightened.

"Oh, Father," she said, "it was only a dream. Forget it. It meant nothing."

Lincoln sighed. "Oh, I know, Mother. I should not have troubled you by telling you about it." He gave a little forced laugh. "I needs get back to my work and not waste time repeating foolish dreams." He got up and left the room.

"I am frightened, Lizzie," said Mrs. Lincoln. "I am very frightened." She gave her head a little shake. "I won't think about bad things." She smiled. "We're going to

Ford's tomorrow night to see a comedy. Should do us both good, and General and Mrs. Grant may go with us."

I got up from my work and slipped out into the hall and then out onto the balcony. Standing there where I had seen the president earlier, I fought to keep from crying. How could I ever forget what I had almost done? "God forgive me," I prayed. "If you will only forgive me, I will show you that I am stronger now. I will go to Wilkes Booth and say that I am glad his plan did not work. I will face him and tell him I am glad Richmond has fallen, that I am not a Southerner at all. I will tell him I do not need his false friendship, and I will write to Steven and beg his forgiveness."

For several days, I tried to keep my promise to God. I went daily to Ford's Theatre to look for Wilkes. "He hasn't been around much," Miss Lillie told me. "He usually comes by more even when we're doing a comedy, like *Our American Cousin*. Wilkes doesn't appear in comedies much, you know. It is tragedy for him, Shakespeare's tragedy mostly. He's a pure tragedian, that one is. If he shows up, though, I'll tell him you are looking for him."

The next day I went to the National Hotel. It took a great deal of courage for me to go to the counter and ask, "Will you tell me, please, what room Mr. J. Wilkes Booth has?"

The man behind the counter smiled at me. "Oh, no, my dear young lady," he said. "We can't give out Mr. Booth's room number. Why, if we did, there would be a constant parade of ladies, young and old, clamoring to see him."

Embarrassed, I stationed myself outside the door to watch, but there was no sight of him. When I grew too weary almost to stand, I made my way toward Ford's Theatre. I would try it again before I gave up and went home.

A workman I had come to know a little was putting away a ladder as I came in the front door. "By chance, have you seen Wilkes Booth around?" I asked.

"Think he was headed toward the shop," he said.

He was here! Facing him with the truth had seemed much easier when I could not find him. I moved to the door left of the stage and made my way down the narrow, dark hall. A sound came from the room in front of me. My hand shook as I reached for the doorknob.

I knew something was different about him as soon as I saw him. It was his eyes. All the familiar softness had left them. Now the darkness of them seemed sinister, frightening. If only I had stopped there in the doorway. If only I had not stepped inside.

By the time he took the gun from his pocket, it was too late to run. He jerked my arm hard, and I cried out in pain. "I don't want to hurt you, Arabella," he said, but I saw no assurance of that in his eyes.

Holding the gun close to me, he let go of my arm. "Take the rope." He pointed to a small piece that hung above the worktable.

Shaking, I did as he said. "Now put your hands

together with the rope between them." Holding the gun with one hand, he used the other hand to wrap the rope around and around my wrists.

"Please, Wilkes, you're hurting me," I said as he pulled hard on the rope.

"So many people have been hurt, sweet Arabella," he said. "Pain doesn't matter much now, not yours, not mine."

He put the gun against my ribs. "We are going to go down into the basement," he said. "You will walk in front of me, and if you make any unexpected moves, I will have to shoot you."

He pushed the gun against me, hard. "Move," he said.

I had never been in the basement, but I knew the stairs behind the stage led to them. Windows in the back of the building were small, and because the hour was around five, what light that did come in was not strong. I gasped when I reached the stairs, and stared down them.

"Be careful, Arabella," Wilkes said. "These steps are steep and made of stone. I am afraid if you slipped, the fall would kill you."

There was a strange, unreal sound to his words. Did he intend to push me? I wondered. I tried to grasp the rail with my bound hands, but I could not do that. Hoping for a little stability, I did rest my hands on top of the rail, as I moved slowly down.

The basement, when finally we reached it, was one large room. Three tiny, grimy windows on the back wall let in dim streaks of light. I could see stage props every-where—dilapidated furniture, some dressing screens, old costumes hanging on racks and stacked on the tables. There were also several big trunks.

"What are you going to do with me?" I asked.

"Hush," said Wilkes. "I'm thinking."

I saw then that he had a length of rope across his shoulders that hung down on both sides in front. Sud-denly, I was certain that he intended to hang me. My eyes searched above me for what he might use. There were some pipes not far above my head.

Wilkes, though, didn't seem to be interested in looking up. Instead he was looking around the basement. "There it is," he said. "I thought there was one down here."

He jabbed the gun into my ribs. "See that chifforobe over there." He motioned with his head. Against the wall beneath the windows, stood the large piece of furniture. "Move," he said, and I walked toward the chifforobe.

It was made of wood and tin. Wilkes shifted the gun to his left hand, and with his right he lifted the latch, and then he tugged at the door. Maybe it won't open, I thought—Oh, God, don't let it open. And at first the door did not budge. Gradually, though, it began to move. Sweat poured down his face, but finally he had it open.

"Get in," he said.

There were drawers in the top part, and beneath them was just enough space for me to stand. "Oh, good," he said, and his voice sounded more familiar, almost normal. "You are a perfect fit."

"Don't make me get in, please," I said.

"Oh, Arabella," he said. "Don't beg. It will only make me feel bad. You don't want me to feel bad, do you?"

"Wilkes," I said, "please."

"Well," he said, "there is one other choice."

"What?" Surely almost anything would be better than being crammed into that musty old chifforobe.

"I could shoot you." He smiled. "Probably that would be kinder." He shrugged his shoulders, then reached out to touch the chifforobe door. "This thing seems pretty tight. I wonder how long you can live in there with such little air?"

"Don't kill me. I am your friend—remember how I tried to help you?"

"Oh, I remember, but you wouldn't want to help me kill the president, would you?"

I swallowed hard. What could I say? Should I agree to be part of his terrible plan? Did I want to live so badly as to agree to help kill Mr. Lincoln?

My face must have revealed my consternation because Wilkes laughed. "Don't fret so, little Arabella. It was only a rhetorical question. I expected no answer. Even if you were willing, there is no part for you to play, not in this drama. You would be nothing to me but a liability. Now I must close this door."

I drew a deep breath into my lungs, but he stopped

and opened the door wide again. I saw him reach for a shirt that lay on a nearby table, and he shoved it toward my mouth. "Open up," he said, and he jabbed the gun into my stomach. "No one is in the building now to hear the shot, but someone might hear you call later."

I opened my mouth, and he pushed the dusty material into it, making me gag. Then he began to push closed the door. I made desperate sounds, trying to beg, but I knew he could not understand. I knew, too, that even if he had understood me, my words would make no difference.

"I am sorry, Arabella," he whispered before the final shove of the door. "In fact, when I am finished drilling a hole in the door of the presidential box, I will come back down if there is time and drill a few holes for you. I have no wish to know you have suffocated. The air will buy you time. Someone may find you before you die from thirst."

The door was closed then, and there was nothing but darkness. I heard the bolt slide. Something wet must have been left inside my prison because a strong mildew smell mixed with the dust that filled my nose.

I strained to listen as Wilkes moved away from me, and then I heard his boots on the stone stairs, climbing. There was not much air. I wondered how long I would last. I wondered if he would come back to drill holes. Pictures of Steven flashed through my mind. If I had to die, I wished mightily that I had been able to tell him how sorry I was for the way I had disappointed him.

I was barely able to breathe by the time I heard the

steps returning. I wanted to make noise, but I did not have the strength. I heard him coming toward me, and then he thumbed around on the outside of the door. There was a scooting sound. I guessed he might be moving something, something on which to stand. "I'll try to make these holes above your head, Arabella," he said. "Perhaps you had best scrunch down as much as possible."

Wiggling, I bent my knees, and just above my head he drilled holes. I could not be sure how many there were, but I began to breathe better. "I'm going now, Arabella," he said. "I don't think you will hear the shot, but probably the commotion afterward. I would imagine there will be a great deal of commotion. When those sounds reach you, you will know Abraham Lincoln is dead."

# 14

# WILKES

## HIS STORY

———◆———

When I finished the holes in the trunk, I was free to go. Would the girl live? Her dark hair, her bright eyes, the pretty shape of her lips . . . would she ever feel the sunlight touch her face again? I had no wish to take her life, but if she were not found until thirst killed her, it would not matter, not really, not in history. And it was history I had to be concerned with.

Oh, yes, Mother, the flames spoke truly—the babe you held will affect his country; that babe grown up will save his country and be blessed by history.

Back at the Surratt house, I climbed the tall front stairs. On the landing, I stood looking at the city of Washington, thinking once more that after tonight I would never see its crowded streets again. I would live the rest of my life in the newly born Confederacy . . . the government that would be reborn after Lincoln's death. I would be adored, but it was not for adoration that I was willing to spill blood, no! Had I not already had the adoration of thousands? I killed for the same reason that Brutus killed, for the same reason Hamlet shed the blood of Claudius, even as Hamlet himself lay dying. I had appeared in all of Shakespeare's plays. No doubt, were he alive, Shakespeare would write his greatest drama about a young actor, a son of the South, who strikes down the despot Lincoln. Ah, 'tis true, many of Shakespeare's heroes died during the last scene. If it 'tis true of me, then so be it. My death is an insignificant matter in the great drama of life.

Inside the house, I went over the details with my small band of followers. My old friends Sam and Michael had gone back to Baltimore. There were but three with me now. They sat on the floor, looking up at me. I moved about, speaking of the glory inherent in what we were about to do. I held out my hands to them and said, "History will bear testimony to our goodness. A grateful people will call our names with love." I could see in the faces of those three that they were with me.

Lewis Powell was to kill Secretary of State William Seward. Because Lewis was unfamiliar with Washington streets, he would need David Herold to guide him and to make sure he got out of the city after the deed. George Atzerod was to kill Vice President Andrew Johnson.

On my way out of the house, I asked Mrs. Surratt to

deliver a package containing guns, whiskey, and a field glass to the tavern that she owned but rented, thirteen miles from Washington City. I did not know how much the woman knew, how much her son told her, before he left town, of our first plan to kidnap the president. I did not question her. I was certain she would never betray us. The other men and I planned to meet at the tavern when our deeds were done.

That evening I dined with my darling Lucy and her parents, who thought she and I were only casual friends. Had I not been trained as an actor, I could not have gotten through the meal without revealing my excitement and fear. Would I ever see her again after tonight? If I did escape to find sanctuary in a rebuilt Confederate nation, would she come to me? Would she be able to stand up to her father, who considered himself a friend of Lincoln's?

We ate oysters and lobster with her parents and a friend of theirs visiting from England. Lucy wore a black silk dress that seemed to be framed by the red velvet of the chair in which she sat. I took out my watch when the meal was done, looked at it, and said, "I must go."

I began, just then, to feel strongly that I was in a play, that I was watching myself on the stage and had no control of how the play ran. I kissed Lucy's hand and murmured some lines from *Hamlet* about how my sins should be remembered in prayer. I suspect she did not understand my quotation much at the time, but later, after she heard, she would understand. And I truly did hope she would pray for me.

I left her then, left the woman I loved to do an act some would consider unforgivable for the South that I loved most of all.

Out on the street, the crowd cheered as the president drove by, and the carriage was slowed by the throngs of people. The newspaper had announced that the Lincolns would attend the performance, and the streets were full of fools who wished to see him, wished to applaud him. So much were they slowed that I was able to get to the theater first. "You won't demand a ticket from me, surely," I said to the ticket taker, and he waved me on with a smile.

I was in the back hall when the president and his party arrived. I did not see them, but when Laura Keene, who was on stage at the time, saw the president enter the nearby box, she stopped her speech. The band began to play "Hail to the Chief."

They got up, every last fool of them, as far as I could see. They stood and clapped for him. Well, I thought, clap loud, for it will be the last time you put your fool hands together for the man.

I looked at my watch again—too long to wait. I would go to a nearby tavern and have a drink. I had several. Well, why not? What I was about to do was not easy. I worried about a guard I had seen outside the door of the hallway that led to the presidential box. I had not expected that. Lincoln frequently went places unguarded. If I shot the soldier at the door, the noise would be a warning. Well, surely the man would recognize me. "The president asked me to stop by," I would say.

During the afternoon I had stored a short length of lumber flat against the inside wall of the hall that led to the president's box. It was the perfect size to slip across the beams of the hallway door, blocking it so that it could not be opened.

"Give me another drink," I said to the bartender. "Too bad," I said to him when he brought it, "that you are not over at Ford's Theatre tonight. I've heard there will be a very special performance."

He smiled. "Why, it can't be too special, Mr. Booth," he said, "being you are not starring in it."

"Thank you, sir," I said when I picked up my glass. "But you see, I do have a part. It is a small appearance, near the end of the show, but I think it is an important part, an important part indeed."

"Must be, sir, or a man like yourself would not be playing the role."

I swallowed down my brandy, left a generous tip, and called, "Good-bye, now," to the barkeeper.

Back in Ford's Theatre, I moved quietly up the stairs. Great joy! The soldier no longer stood guard at the door. First, I bolted the hall door. Then I bent to look through the peephole I had made that afternoon. I could see clearly into the box. The other man sat on a couch. Mrs. Lincoln and the woman guest sat in straight chairs. Lincoln was in

a rocking chair. Very good, I thought, he has rocked himself and is about to sleep.

I knew the play, knew when laughs would cover
sounds. When the laugh I waited for came, I slipped inside.
I waited for the next big laugh, quickly took the revolver
from my pocket, aimed, and fired.

It took the others in the box a few moments to realize
what had happened. Then Mrs. Lincoln screamed. The
other man—I later learned his name was Major Rath-
bone—spotted me and tried to grab hold of me.

I dropped my gun and drew my knife. I remember
laughing loudly as I slashed his arm. Strange, I think I
saw a glimpse of his bone as my knife carved into his arm.
Surprised and bleeding, he fell back. I vaulted myself up
to the ledge of the box, so that I could jump to the stage
below.

Jumps were no problem to me. I frequently made
them in the course of a play, and the box was not far above
the stage. It was that flag! That cursed Union flag caught
my foot as I jumped, and I did not land straight. A pierc-
ing pain shot through my foot and leg, but I did not let it
slow me.

I turned to the audience. It was my finest hour onstage. No one outside the box yet knew of the shot, but still
every eye was on me. More than fifteen hundred people
had crowded into that theater that night to see the president, but now every eye was on me.

I raised my bloody knife in the air and shouted, "Sic

semper tyrannis!" It was the Latin motto of Virginia, the state I considered my home because Maryland had not seceded, and it meant, "Thus always with tyrants!"

Then I ran off the stage, through the back curtains, past the questioning faces of actors to the backdoor. "Hold this horse for me," I told a stagehand earlier in the evening. "He is too spirited, and will break loose if I try to tie him." I gave the man a goodly sum of money, so I knew the horse would be where I left it and ready to go.

Even with my leg paining me, I was able to jump on the horse. I grabbed the reins and was moving away when I heard shouts of "Stop him! He has shot the president." The words filled me with an elation such as I had never felt even when being applauded by great crowds. It was done!

The horse was a fast one, and I urged him on. "The Choctaws are after us," I said to him as I used to say to my pony Cola. For three miles we moved with no interruptions. Then the Eleventh Street Bridge loomed before me, guarded by soldiers. During the war the bridge had been closed to all traffic after sundown, but regulations had been lax since the surrender.

I pulled my horse to a stop, drew in a breath, and told myself to remain calm. There had been no time for news of my deed to reach this man.

"Who are you?" he asked.

"My name is Booth," I told him, and in my mind I added, A name you will know well before this night is done.

"Why are you traveling?"

"I had business in Washington City and am returning home to Maryland."

"What town?"

I told him that I lived in the country in Charles County. He told me that I was not supposed to use the bridge after nine, but when I explained that I had not known about the rule, he allowed me to cross.

On, on, I rode. At Soper's Hill, about eight miles from Washington City, I met Davy Herold. He had been able to get out of the city after being separated from Lewis Powell. Herold told me, though, that Powell hadn't got the job done with Seward, only injured him. Others in the household had interfered.

Davy also related the bad news that he had seen Atzerod drunk in the streets after he pawned the gun he was to have used to kill Andrew Johnson. I was disappointed that neither the vice president nor the secretary of state had been struck down, but I could not be too low. Not with the success I had just had with Lincoln.

"No matter," I told him, and I saw the worried look lift from his face. He cares only for my approval, I thought, and I told him he did well. I told him too about my leg. "The pain is almost unbearable," I said, "but we must ride on."

We rode first to the tavern to pick up the guns, whiskey, and field glass Mrs. Surratt had delivered for us.

Davy went inside. I did not get down from the horse. We rode on into the night.

The pain grew worse. I no longer thought of the soldiers who must be riding behind us. The throbbing took away all other thoughts, and the pain in my back was now as bad as that in my leg. I pulled my horse to a stop. "Dr. Mudd is nearby," I told Davy. "I must have help." I had been there in his house, had spent the night there and sat at his table. Surely he would aid me.

Mudd was reluctant, but he examined me. He asked no questions, but I think he knew what I had done. He stroked his beard and delivered the bad news. "Broken, two inches above the ankle." I thought of the cursed flag that had caused my injury.

The doctor set my leg and gave me something for the pain. I slept once more in a bed beneath his roof. The next morning he had a servant make crutches for me.

The doctor was anxious for us to leave, but his wife protested. "Mr. Booth shouldn't travel in that condition," she said.

"We won't go far if he is in pain," said Davy, who was smart enough to know we must be on the road.

I wanted newspapers, wanted to read the words of praise in Southern newspapers. We came across a man named Jones who said he would take us across the river at night. He also said he would bring food and newspapers. I wanted papers more than food. We hid in the weeds, waiting for dark. Waiting for the newspapers. We lay on our backs on the damp earth. Fever racked my body. The sky above me seemed at times to reach down to take me up into it.

When finally the papers came, I read, and cried out in pain. My pain was worse then than any pain caused by my swollen, discolored leg, far greater than the aches from the fever that racked my poor body. I read, and a deep pain came from my heart. All the papers denounced what I had done. Not one spoke of me as a brave patriot, not one.

The Richmond paper hurt worst of all, calling my act the heaviest blow ever to come to the people of the South. I drew in my breath, but wait—perhaps those first words were the result of the fever. Perhaps my eyes saw things that were not there. I sat up, leaning on one elbow. No! The words were really there. Jefferson Davis, they said, had talked of how the man who had done this cowardly act must be a crazy man, who thought he was acting in defense of the South but who was really the worst enemy of the Southern people.

The worst enemy of the South! How could they say such things of me, who had thought nothing of my own safety, who had been chased like a common criminal, chased with dogs and guns through swamps? Where was the praise? Where were the people who should be applauding what I had done? The fever rose in my brain. "Water," I whispered to the man who had ridden with me. He put water to my lips, and I could see him plainly for a moment, a simple young man who followed after me as a child might.

I strained to remember his name, and it came to me, Davy. "It was for nothing," I said to him. "Useless, Davy, absolutely useless." Then his face floated up and away from me into the sky.

I wanted to write of what I had done. In my pocket was an appointment book from last year, from 1864. It was small, but its pages gave me a place to write. My head cleared, and I wrote quickly, fearing the confusion of fever would return. I wrote words to justify what I had done. I wrote that were I to go back to Washington City and be allowed to speak, I could clear my name of wrongdoing. I wrote about how our country owed all its troubles to him. I wrote that I did not repent what I had done. God, I said, had simply made me the instrument of his punishment. I wrote that it was for God to judge me, not man.

When I was finished, I slipped the book back into the pocket of my coat. The mist from the nearby water seemed to connect to the sky, and it came to me that I was not really lying on the ground, staring up at water. This was, I remembered finally, only a play, a play about a terrible man who had led a people down dark paths. Someone had to come to kill the leader, and that person was the star of the play. Of course, the part was mine. Who else could play the role so well as I? It was not a Shakespearean play, but the tone was like Shakespeare's. My life had been spent among Shakespeare's words; always I had heard those words from my father, from my brothers, from my own lips. Of course it would be I who starred in this Shake-speare-like play.

The scene changed. The boy Davy, who had been given the role of my helper, and I were in a boat in the night. In the night, Davy lost his direction, and we ended up on the same shore from which we had started.

A man named Garrett was kind to us. We slept in his house, and he gave us food, but the troops were near, and Garrett grew afraid, said we had to leave. Then he felt sympathy for us and let us sleep in the tobacco barn.

And so we were there among the leftover smells of the tobacco leaves that were harvested in the fall, hung in the barn, and then taken to market. There were tobacco knives on the wall with large curved blades, but they would do us no good.

"Come out," the soldiers shouted.

"No," I explained to Davy. "Our part calls for us to refuse to surrender."

The soldiers set the barn on fire. Flames licked up around us, and Davy Herold began to cry. Poor thing, he had forgotten that this was a play. "A man wants to come out," I called to those who played the soldiers, and Davy left the barn.

Flames licked at the walls, making the interior of the barn, which had been dark, light as day. "I will never sur-render," I shouted. I had no wish to be taken alive, to die like a criminal. God, I prayed, spare me that. I have too great a soul to die in such a base way.

As if in answer to my prayer the bullet came through the crack, and it struck my neck.

They came inside then and dragged me forth to lie upon the porch of the house. They gave me water, and they waited, as did I, for death to come, for death to come with its final curtain on the drama that has been my life.

A straw mattress was brought to the porch. They placed me on the bed and put a cloth dampened with brandy against my lips. "Tell my mother I died for my country," I said, and I slipped into unconsciousness, the images of my life flickering as the flames had flickered around me. I lingered for some time, then woke and asked to see my hands. A soldier held them up before my eyes. "Useless," I whispered. "Useless." Then the lights went out in the theater.

# 15

# ARABELLA

## HER STORY

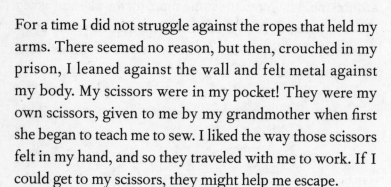

For a time I did not struggle against the ropes that held my arms. There seemed no reason, but then, crouched in my prison, I leaned against the wall and felt metal against my body. My scissors were in my pocket! They were my own scissors, given to me by my grandmother when first she began to teach me to sew. I liked the way those scissors felt in my hand, and so they traveled with me to work. If I could get to my scissors, they might help me escape.

I began to strain against the ropes, forcing my arms to separate over and over as far as possible. Each time my bonds felt slightly more loose, and my hopes grew. If I could get out of this trunk, I would run, crying out what was about to happen. As I worked at the ropes, I heard the sound of feet above me, people filling the theater.

Then came laughter. The play had begun, but that would not stop me from running onto the stage, screaming my warning to Mr. Lincoln.

Push, push, push, I told myself, and I felt the sting of rope cutting into my flesh. Next there was a dampness that I knew must be my blood. What part of my wrists did the blood come from? I had heard of people who died from cutting their own wrists, but the thought did not slow my work. Probably I would die here anyway, unable to scream for help. I would die from lack of water and from shame for having been such a fool as to let my head be turned by a handsome man with a smooth voice.

Finally, I thought the ropes might be loose enough to pull out one hand. Gritting my teeth, I tugged with every ounce of my strength. My hand was free, and the ropes fell to my feet. First I yanked the filthy gag from my mouth. "Help! Help me, please!" I screamed, but I knew no one would hear me.

I wanted to rest, but there was no time. I had to get to work. My right hand went immediately to my pocket, and my fingers closed on the scissors.

With my left hand, I touched the inside of my prison door. The holes Wilkes had drilled were too high for me to reach, but I searched for some other place to dig at with my scissors. Despite the darkness, I closed my eyes, trying to remember where the bolt fastened the door on the outside. If I were to escape, I would need to make a hole near that bolt.

In my mind I could picture the fastener. It was, I believed, near the middle of the chifforobe. I had stared at it, thinking that the iron bolt was thick, too strong to be broken by my weight thrown against the inside. It could be slid, though. If the hole could be made big enough for my hand, for my arm to reach through, the bolt could be moved, and putting the scissors back in my pocket, I began to use both hands to feel the door of my prison in the estimated area of the lock.

Wonderful! There was a small round spot where perhaps a screw or a hook had been. Retrieving my scissors, I opened the blades and pushed one against the hole, digging, digging. It was slow work, but the hole began to be bigger, large enough now so that the tip of my smallest finger could go into it.

How long will it take me to make a hole big enough to get my arm through? It could be hours, maybe days. A sob started up from inside me, but I held it in as if I were still gagged. Don't go to pieces now, I told myself. You have to try. I began to dig against the tin.

Above my head the play and the audience's laughter continued. Nothing had happened yet. Wilkes had said that I would know when the president was shot. There was still time. The hole was big enough now to be in the wooden part of the door. I began to tear at it with my hands. Pieces of wood stuck me, but I did not slow. Maybe I could get my hand through. I shoved with all my strength, my skin burning against the wood. I drew in a great breath and lunged once more. Splinters cut at my arm, but finally my hot fingers touched the cool iron bolt.

Just then the sounds above me changed. A scream came to my ears. "It's part of the play," I said aloud, but I knew better. Screams echoed above me. Over and over I heard screams and running feet. For a moment I leaned against the back wall, my body shaking. It was too late. I knew the president had been shot, shot well, no doubt. Wilkes Booth was not a man who did a job halfway. Perhaps I should stop my efforts to undo the bolt. Would it not be better for me to die here than to live always with the shame of how I had lost all reason?

Slowly I closed my fingers over the bolt and slid it. A big push made the door swing open with a creak. The basement was dark, but a light from the hall above seeped through the crack at the stairway door. Bumping against old tables, chairs, and other discarded furniture, I made my way toward the light.

At the top, I drew in a deep breath and stepped out into the house. Colors blurred before my eyes. Crowds of ladies in colorful gowns and men in black evening wear pressed toward the front. There were too many of them between me and the door. I leaned for a few minutes against the back of an empty seat, but I had to see what had happened to Mr. Lincoln. I turned back and went behind the stage, where only a few people had sought the back exit.

Soldiers guarded the door, and one of them stood

questioning two stagehands. No one tried to stop me. I moved quickly down the steps. Then I ran. Holding up my skirts, I raced around the block to get to the front of the building.

In front, soldiers used their swords to mark the pathway that must be cleared. "Step back," shouted an officer. "Step back or I'll run you through." The crowd moved back. I could see him then, carried by six soldiers. His long arms were folded over his chest, and his eyes were closed.

"We will need a carriage to get him to the White House, doctor," the officer said to a young man in evening clothes who walked beside the soldiers.

"No," the doctor said, "he wouldn't live to get there. There's a boardinghouse across the street."

"He isn't dead," I said to myself. "He isn't dead." But the doctor had said he couldn't survive the trip to the White House.

Mrs. Lincoln came from the building then, helped by two women, to walk behind the soldiers. She came to follow the men who carried her husband across the street and up the steps of the boardinghouse. She was sobbing. I stared at her white dress with red flowers and remembered the day Mrs. Keckley had fitted it, the day Mr. Lincoln told his dream.

For a while I stood there across the street from where they had taken the president. I leaned against the bricks of Ford's Theatre and wrapped my arms around my body as if to hold myself together. Groups of people stood about, talking. Some of them were kneeling in prayer. Soldiers were everywhere, and after a time they began to call, "Go to your homes. Nothing more can be done. Clear the streets." It had started to rain, and I walked home wet and cold.

My grandmother roused from her sleep when I came in. "You're terrible late, child," she said.

I did not want to disturb her sleep with the terrible news. "I stayed long with the Lincolns," I said, and she went back to sleep. I did not light a lamp. Undressing in the dark, I marveled at how unchanged things were. I laid my wet clothing across the same familiar rocking chair. I lay down in the same bed, the one I had slept in every night since I was eight years old. Outside my window, I could see the moon, unchanged from last night, and the same bird called, just as he had last night. How could all these things be exactly as they had always been when inside me all organs had changed to stone?

They say he died at 7:22 the next morning. They say that when his heart beat for the last time, the minister Reverend Phineas Gurley prayed about God's will being done and that Mr. Hay, his personal secretary, noticed a look of great peace came to his worn face. They say Secretary of War Stanton raised his hands and said, "Now he belongs to the ages."

Shortly after he died, church bells began to toll just as they had to announce the end of the war. Those bells, though, had been joyful. These were slow and rang mournfully across the rooftops of Washington City.

I dressed quickly and went out to the street. Next door, our neighbors were hanging black crepe around their windows. I wandered about the streets, and it was the same everywhere, homes and businesses draped in black, a city in mourning.

The newspapers that day were edged with black. I bought one from a boy on a corner and stared down at a likeness of Wilkes. A $50,000 reward was offered to anyone who could lead authorities to him. The article described John Wilkes Booth as five feet seven inches tall, with dark eyes and dark hair. There was no mention of the power in his soft voice or of the magic in his smile.

They laid our president's body in the East Room. The casket sat on a raised platform with an arched canopy, just as it had in Mr. Lincoln's dream. Grandmother went with me, leaning heavily on my arm. I was glad for the need to support her, and I think that without that duty, I might have fallen in a faint when I looked on his face.

The train that bore his body back to Illinois for burial also took the coffin of Willie. It had been taken from the Washington City cemetery so that it could be buried again next to his father's. I, along with thousands of others, watched the train leave our city on April 21. A funeral had been held in Washington, and eleven more would be held in cities where the train stopped.

I read in the newspaper that more than seven million Americans waited with bowed heads to see the funeral train or view the body. They mourned him, I know, those millions, and I also knew they did it without the guilt I felt.

Ford's Theatre stayed closed, and of course, there would be no more dressmaking work done for Mrs. Lincoln at the White House. I was left with no way to support my grandmother and myself, but for days I was too weak to make plans.

Eleven days after the president died, Wilkes Booth too lost his life. I hated what he had done, hated the way I let myself be swayed from reason by his charms. Yet I could not hate him. I sat at our small table and stared at his likeness in the newspaper I had put there.

My grandmother came to look over my shoulder. "Looks like a nice young man," she said, her voice full of wonder, "hardly more than a boy." She bent closer. "Strange to see a devil look so normal."

"I saw him at Ford's a few times," I said softly.

My grandmother made a clicking noise with her tongue. "Tisk tisk," she said. "Thank the Lord you never took up with him."

I heard later when I saw Miss Lillie from Ford's that Lucy Hale, daughter of an important man, had been allowed to view Wilkes's body and to snip a piece of hair from his head to keep as a remembrance. "It makes me marvel," Miss Lillie said, "to think he had such a sweet smile."

I could tell no one about my burden of guilt, but the secret weighed heavily on me, eating, it seemed, a hole through my insides. I missed Steven terribly, longed to ask his forgiveness, longed to discuss my guilt with him, but if I wrote to ask his forgiveness, I would have to explain why I had turned my back on our chance to spend time together. How could I ever explain? I feared I had lost Steven.

Finally I had to think about making money, and I decided to go to Grover's Theatre. Tad Lincoln had been attending a performance of *Aladdin and the Magic Lamp* there with his tutor on the night his father was shot. Standing outside the big building, I did not feel shy. Perhaps shyness belonged to the girl I had been, not the sad young woman I had become.

"I worked at Ford's Theatre in the costume shop," I told the manager after I introduced myself, "and I had been promised a small part as soon as one came along."

The man put down the pen with which he had been writing when I came into the room. He looked at me with doubt. "The actors and employees of Ford's have all been arrested." It was true, the Ford's people had all been taken in for prolonged questioning.

"I was only an occasional worker, in exchange for tickets. They did not send for me." I shrugged, glanced down for a moment, then brought my gaze back to rest on his face. "I worked full-time at the White House as a helper to Mrs. Lincoln's dressmaker."

"Ah," he said. "I see. Both sources of employment are now denied to you." He stood. "Your luck is good today, Arabella. Our costume mistress just took off with an actor who has gone to New York."

It was a big job. My fingers and my mind were kept busy, but as I sewed, I remembered what I had done. For three months, I worked hard at the theater, and in late July I was given a small part in a comedy, a servant girl who said four words onstage. I was happy, but still a heavy weight hung in my heart.

I decided one morning before work that I would write a letter to Steven. Remembering his face on that terrible day, I doubted if our relationship could be restored, but still I had to try, had to make an effort to apologize. I took a piece of paper and a pen. "Dear Steven," I wrote. "Please forgive me for not making time to see you. I was in a terrible state and still am. I have made some bad decisions. Perhaps someday I will be able to tell you about them. I have missed your letters. Your friend, Bella."

I posted the letter and when enough days had passed, I began to hope for a response. None came. In late August, as I said my four words, my eyes fell on the audience. Could I be seeing correctly, or was I blinded by the lights into only thinking I saw Steven there?

Yes, I was certain it was my old friend, three rows back and near the center. I left the stage feeling shaky. He had planned to come to Washington in August. How long had he been in the city? He had not come to see me. I imagined his surprise when I appeared in the play. At least he had not gotten up and walked out when I came onto the stage. I had prayed for a chance to see him, but now I felt afraid.

Unwilling to run into him, I stayed backstage longer than I usually did when the production was over. I was about to make my way to the backdoor when I heard his voice. "Bella," he called, and I whirled to see him standing there, watching me.

For a moment, we looked at each other, neither of us moving. Then very slowly I began to walk toward him. "So you did come to Washington City before going to Harvard?" I said, and he nodded. "You never answered my letter," I said.

"I was too angry." He sighed and shrugged his shoulders. "I guess I still am angry, but I wanted to see you, wanted to hear what you had to say. Your grandmother told me you were here."

We walked out of the theater into the Washington night, and I began to talk. "I was beguiled," I said, drawing in a breath, "beguiled by a beautiful demon named Booth."

A small cry came from Steven when I said the name, but we walked on. And as we walked, my story came pouring out. I held back nothing. I told how I was charmed by Wilkes's voice and by his smile. I told about the red dress, and how I had felt like Cinderella with her prince. I told him that even while I did what I did, I knew I was acting like a fool, that what I felt for Wilkes was not real. I cried as I talked about that last night, about seeing Mr. Lincoln being carried from Ford's Theatre. We had stopped in a small park, and we sat on a bench beneath a hydrangea bush.

"Here." Steven handed me his handkerchief. It was too dark to see his face, but his voice held no warmth.

"Do you hate me now?" I asked.

He did touch my hand then. "I could never hate you, Bella. I'm stunned. I can't deny that. Of all the things I thought, I never imagined—"

"Well," I said, "you may not be able to hate me, but I certainly hate myself." I heard myself saying aloud what had only briefly crossed my mind. "I think I need to confess. I want to tell Mr. Stanton what happened."

"Confess? Oh, no." Steven sat up straight, alarmed. In July four of the people involved with Wilkes had been hanged. One of them, Mrs. Surratt, was the first woman ever executed by the American government. Three others, including the doctor who treated Wilkes, had been sent to prison. "You must not confess. It's far too dangerous," he said.

I reached for a purple flower and pressed it between my fingers. "I have to do it. I don't think I can heal until I've told the truth."

"I'll go with you," he said, and I felt better. If Steven still cared enough to be concerned about my confessing, I had hope for our relationship.

"I am afraid of punishment," I said, "but not as afraid

as I am of losing you." I picked another flower. "I can't bear the thought that I might have lost your trust and affection." A shudder passed through my body. "How could I have been foolish enough to throw our closeness away?"

Steven had touched my hand before, but now he wrapped his fingers over mine. "You haven't lost me, Bella. I'll be with you whatever happens."

Steven was in Washington for only one more day. We decided to see Secretary Stanton the next morning in his office at the War Department Building. "We have information about the assassination," Steven told the soldier stationed outside his door, and we were ushered in.

I had often seen Secretary Stanton in the White House. Now he was behind a high desk, the sort that required standing. He faced the entrance of the room, and I felt his spectacled eyes bore into me as we came in the door.

"My name is Arabella Getchel," I told him.

To my surprise he smiled at me. "You are the girl who helped with Mrs. Lincoln's sewing, aren't you?"

He was a man who had trained his eye to be ever observant. "Yes," I said, "and I have a terrible story to tell you." Steven reached out then and took my hand.

While I talked I looked directly into Mr. Stanton's face. If I were to be arrested and put into prison, then so be it. I wanted only to free myself of guilt, and I held tightly to Steven. All through my story, Mr. Stanton watched me intently. He had a full black beard that was grizzled with gray and an odd streak of silver hair on his chin.

When I was finished, Mr. Stanton removed his glasses, rubbed his eyes, and looked away from us for a moment. Then he turned back. "The strain has been too much for you, young lady," he said. "Your imagination has taken over your mind. The idea that a fiend like Booth would rely on an innocent girl, no more than a child—" He shook his head. "This tragedy has exhausted us all and done peculiar things to many a mind. Go home, my dear, and pray to God for guidance."

I opened my mouth to protest, but Steven spoke first. "Thank you, sir," he said, and he led me from the room. In the dark hall, I started again to say something, but Steven shook his head and put his finger to his lips.

Neither of us spoke till we were outside. A cool breeze lifted the hair that had matted on my forehead with sweat. "Steven," I said, "he didn't believe me. I need to go back."

He took my hand again. "No," he said. "You did what was right." He pressed his lips together before he went on. "I am not at all sure that he doubted what you said." He shook his head. "No, I am almost certain he did believe you. But he wanted to find a way to let you go. What purpose would be served by locking you up and dragging you through a trial? No, the man has given you a way out, Bella. Take it."

I worked for a few hours that morning in the costume shop at Grover's, but Steven and I spent the afternoon walking the streets of Washington City together as we had when we were younger. He bought me a yellow rose from a girl on a street corner, and I fastened it into my hair.

I felt that Steven had forgiven me, but I experienced no return of the easy carefree feeling we used to share. I wondered if I would ever feel really good again. Maybe those experiences belonged to the children we had been before the darkness. At the train depot, I remembered that day he had run back to kiss me.

This time he kissed me before he walked away. "Tell me you've forgiven me," I said.

He nodded. "I have. I love you, Bella." He smiled, the same old Steven. "Always have, always will."

I stood on the platform watching the train until it disappeared from sight. Suddenly I did feel light. My heart sang. I had Steven back. He knew the terrible truth about what I had done, and amazingly he had truly forgiven me.

On my walk home, I enjoyed looking about me at my home, Washington City. I would write to my father soon. I wanted him to have a letter from me waiting for him when he got home. I would tell him that I loved him and would so enjoy a visit with him. I would explain, though, that I had no wish to live in Richmond again. I could not leave my grandmother or Washington City.

I turned toward Tenth Street. I wanted to see Ford's Theatre again. I had just stopped in front when Mr. John Ford came to unlock the door. He remembered my name. "Hello, Bella," he said. "I'm glad they didn't drag you into their awful questioning." He put in his key. "I've only today been given the right to go back inside." He shook his head. "Don't know what will happen to the place."

"Mr. Ford," I said. "Could I go in?" I swallowed hard. "For just a minute? I'd like to see . . ."

He turned back to look at me. "Well," he said, "if you won't go telling anyone. All kinds of folks would be after me for a look."

"I won't," I said, "I promise," and I followed him into the dark building.

"I'll see to a few lights and go to my office. You just leave when you're ready."

After some of the gaslights were on, I could see the aftermath of the horrible scene. Programs lay everywhere, dropped by running people. There were bloodstains on the stairs, and I went into the president's box, where the rocking chair stood empty. I looked down at the stage and saw a tear in the green carpet where Wilkes had landed. I leaned against the ledge of the box and took one last look. I remembered Mr. Lincoln, the worn lines of his face and the warmth of his eyes. I remembered Wilkes. What gifts he had, what power to lead those around him! What he might have been if only the twisted, angry part had not taken control! I would never be the same for having known him, but his ghost would not haunt me. I left the dimness of Ford's Theatre. Out on the streets of Washington City the sun was bright.

# Author's Note

Writing about John Wilkes Booth was the idea of my husband, John, but I loved the suggestion as soon as I heard it. Years earlier, I had stood in the Washington, D.C., building that had been the boardinghouse where Abraham Lincoln died. Touching the pillow on which his head had rested sent a strange sensation through my body. I remember wondering then about the man who shot the great leader. I knew only the killer's name and that he was an actor.

Learning about Booth was fascinating. I read several books, including *John Wilkes Booth: A Sister's Memoir*, by Asia Booth Clarke. Asia wrote the book in England, where she lived the rest of her life to escape the disgrace associated with the Booth name. No one wanted to hear anything at all good about John Wilkes Booth, and the book was not published until 1938, long after Asia's death. Asia loved her brother, as did his other siblings.

Everything I wrote about Booth's early life and about his brothers and sisters is true. His mother really did think she had a vision about his future, and he really did have the frightening experience with the fortune-teller. Asia also wrote all about Booth's joining the soldiers who guarded John Brown and her brother's reaction to that event.

Lucy Hale interested me a great deal. I wonder if she and John Wilkes Booth would ever have married if he had lived. I imagined most of the scenes between Lucy and Booth, but she really was a friend of Robert Lincoln's. Booth did dine with Lucy and her parents the evening that he shot the President. I was touched by the fact that Lucy wrote down the lines from the poem "Maud Muller" and gave them to Booth. "For of all sad words of tongue or pen, The saddest are these. It might have been" certainly fit the relationship between Lucy and Wilkes. How shocked and hurt she must have been after the man she loved fired those terrible shots.

Did Booth really catch his foot in the flag, causing him to land badly on the stage and injure himself? Most books I read said he did. A recently published one, however, contained the theory that the injury came later. We will probably never know for sure.

We do know the words Booth wrote in the little book he carried. We know he did think he would be praised in Southern papers for what he had done. In reality he died just as he did in this story, after saying, "Useless. Useless." He was buried secretly by the government, but eventually his body was returned to his family and was put in the family plot in a Baltimore cemetery. People often throw pennies on his grave because that coin has Lincoln's picture on it.

Research for this book also taught me a great deal about Abraham Lincoln and his family. Things have certainly changed in Washington since the days when Mr. Lincoln often rode down the dirt streets alone and anyone could wait in line to see him at the White House. He really did have the dream about his death, and reading about his account of that dream brought tears to my eyes. I enjoyed learning more about Elizabeth Keckley, the former slave who became dressmaker and friend to Mary Lincoln.

The Lincolns had lost their second-born son, four-year-old Edward, before they went to Washington. As in this book, Willie died during his father's presidency at the age of eleven. Tad, the youngest of Lincoln's four sons, died when he was eighteen. Only Robert, who became a lawyer and statesman, lived a long life. What I wrote about Lincoln's sons was true. I imagined the poem for Bella, but Willie Lincoln did write the one about Colonel Baker and have it published in the newspaper. Willie and Tad did have a black-and-white goat named Nanko, and Robert Lincoln actually was saved by Edwin Booth from being killed by a train.

Before that night in Ford's Theatre, no American

president had ever been assassinated. The country was shocked. Even in the South, where people did not like Lincoln, most realized that the former Confederate states would have had an easier time coming back into the Union if the president had lived. In the frenzy to find and punish all the conspirators, even Jefferson Davis, president of the Confederacy, was brought to trial, but he was found to be innocent.

Arabella Getchel is a fictitious character, but she became very real to me. She is the mirror that reflects the people, events, and surroundings of that memorable period of history. Ernest Hemingway once said, "All good books are alike in that they are truer than if they really happened, and after you are finished reading one you will feel that all that happened to you." I hope *Assassin* makes you feel that you lived in Washington City with Bella.

ANNA MYERS has written numerous books for Walker & Company, including her most recent novels *Wart*, *Confessions from the Principal's Chair*, *Hoggee*, and *Tulsa Burning*. She has earned many accolades for her work. *Tulsa Burning* was selected as a New York Public Library's Book for the Teen Age, and *Assassin* won Anna her third Oklahoma Book Award for Children's Books. Anna lives in Tulsa, Oklahoma.

Visit her Web site at www.annamyers.info.

# EXPERIENCE THE LIGHTER SIDE OF ANNA MYERS...

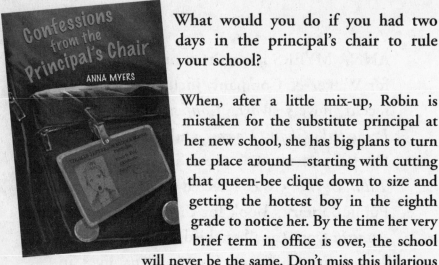

What would you do if you had two days in the principal's chair to rule your school?

When, after a little mix-up, Robin is mistaken for the substitute principal at her new school, she has big plans to turn the place around—starting with cutting that queen-bee clique down to size and getting the hottest boy in the eighth grade to notice her. By the time her very brief term in office is over, the school will never be the same. Don't miss this hilarious middle-school mix-up, *Confessions from the Principal's Chair.*

## And coming soon ...

Experience laughs of magical proportions in Anna Myer's forthcoming novel *Wart* ...

Wanda Gibbs is no ordinary substitute teacher—from the moment she arrived, Stewart has had a bad feeling about her. He soon finds out she might be a witch and is threatening to use her magic on him! Can they strike a truce before Stewart ends up as a frog?